resurrection

By the same author

The Wereling trilogy
Wounded
Prey
Resurrection

The Thieves trilogy
Thieves Like Us
The Aztec Code
The Bloodline Cipher

THE WERELING
resurrection

BLOOMSBURY

LONDON BERLIN NEW YORK

Bloomsbury Publishing, London, Berlin and New York

First published in Great Britain in 2004 by Bloomsbury Publishing Plc
36 Soho Square, London, W1D 3QY

This edition first published in 2009

A CIP catalogue record of this book is available from the British Library

ISBN 978 0 7475 9968 5

The paper this book is printed on is certified independently in accordance
with the rules of the FSC. It is ancient-forest friendly.
The printer holds chain of custody.

FSC
Mixed Sources
Product group from well-managed
forests and other controlled sources

Cert no. SGS - COC - 2061
www.fsc.org
© 1996 Forest Stewardship Council

Typeset by Dorchester Typesetting Group Ltd
Printed in Great Britain by Clays Ltd, St Ives plc

10 9 8 7 6 5 4 3 2 1

www.bloomsbury.com/childrens

To my parents, Wendy and Tony Cole,
with love and gratitude

CHAPTER ONE

This is how it ends, Kate Folan thought.

She'd run into a blind alley. There was no way out, and her pursuers were right behind her. 'Tom!' she yelled, clutching the stitch in her side. 'Tom, where are you?'

The biting Chicago wind seemed to snatch the words from her lips. No answer came back to her. All she heard was her breath as it came in sharp ragged gasps, clouding out into the freezing December air.

Kate wished desperately that Tom were here. When they'd realised the gang was following them, they'd fled, splitting up in the hope of confusing them. The gang had gone after Tom – but then a car had come out of nowhere and picked up *her* trail.

Smoothing long straggles of hair from her clammy forehead, Kate looked around frantically for somewhere to hide – someplace she'd overlooked.

There was nowhere.

The car slowly drew up, filling the entire alleyway, its headlights blinding her.

Then with a quiet click the driver's door opened.

'Stay away from me,' Kate gasped.

Her words were answered with a hunting roar, followed by the hard smack of something heavy on metal.

A shadowy creature, sleek and sinewy, was now crouched on the hood of the car. It was somewhere between a wolf and a man, deep-chested and covered in dark, lustrous fur, its sharp ivory teeth bared.

Kate screamed and shrank away as the creature pounced towards her. But as it landed at her feet, she saw that its eyes were deep brown, soulful. Human eyes, that had resisted changing to the evil yellow glint of pure lupine. It was Tom. She fell to her knees beside him. 'You found me,' she breathed.

Tom turned his glance to the car blocking their way and roared defiantly, then shattered one of its glaring headlights with a swipe of his club-like paw.

Kate guessed his encounter with the gang must have brought on Tom's lupine change. But she wondered uneasily how he had dealt with his attackers.

The car door opened. Kate heard a familiar rough English voice.

'You stupid hairy sod, Tom Anderson. This is a hire car and I've got no accidental damage cover.'

'Blood?' Kate called out in disbelief.

'*Out* for blood, the trouble you two have put me to.'

The owner of the voice climbed out of the driver's seat into full view. Adam Blood. Tall and clean-cut, in a heavy black overcoat; a rueful half-smile on his handsome face, snowflakes catching on his dark floppy hair.

Tom relaxed his fighting stance and sank back on his haunches.

'You scared me half to death!' Kate yelled at Blood. She shook her head, words spilling out of her mouth in a great flood of relief. 'First of all you arrange to meet us and then don't show. Then we get chased through the streets by a gang. And ...' She slammed her hand down on the dented car hood. 'And then *you* come after me in *this* thing!'

'You ran so damned fast, I wanted to make sure I didn't lose you!' Blood protested. 'You two have been bloody hard to find!'

'Well, congrats. You did it. In the end.' Half-slipping in the snow, Kate went forward and grabbed Blood in a clumsy embrace. 'Thanks,' she said, shivering with cold and shock.

'This kind of thanks I can handle,' he murmured, his breath warming her ear as he hugged her back. 'But Tom's not going to jump up and lick me, is he?'

'Ha ha.' She glanced behind her. Tom was lying down now. With the immediate danger passed, his human self would soon begin to reassert control. 'I thought you were never going to show,' she hissed into Blood's neck reproachfully.

'Ditto. But do you really think I'd miss out on a jolly Christmas reunion, Trolly?'

Kate smiled. Trolly was short for Troll Lover, the alias she always used online. Troll Lover was the only name he'd had for her for almost two years, and he still liked to use it.

To Kate, it felt like a name from another lifetime.

As she clung to Blood, exhausted, the scent of his expensive cologne took her back to the time she'd finally met him in the flesh in New Orleans, and those first frightening days on the run. Once the head of a misfit group keeping tabs on the dark, supernatural side of the city, he had become a good friend to her and Tom. More than that, he'd saved their lives.

'Come on,' said Blood, extricating himself from her hug. 'It's brass monkeys out here. Get in the car and I'll take you to whatever fleapit you're staying in.'

'We've got a place in Uptown,' Kate told him, 'and yes, it *is* a fleapit, but I can't wait to get back there. Thanks for the lift.'

'You're welcome. And you are too, Tom, as long as you're not moulting...' He trailed off, peering over Kate's shoulder. 'Oh.'

Kate turned and saw that Tom had transformed back to his human form. A little sting went through her at the sight of his naked body face down in the slushy snow, slim and muscular. 'He'll freeze to death,' she muttered to Blood. 'Give me your coat.'

'Just call me Santa,' sighed Blood, unbuttoning his heavy overcoat. 'Three days early.'

Kate took the coat. Her face felt fiery as she crouched down and wrapped it around Tom, who was starting to shiver. He looked up at her, his brown eyes glinting under his dark brows, hair damp and spiky. She just wanted to gather him up and hold him close. Not like a friend, not in the way she'd just hugged Blood, but ...

Don't go there, she told herself, rising back up and helping Tom to his bare feet.

'Those assholes had me trapped,' he muttered through chattering teeth. 'They herded me into an alleyway, then ...'

Kate shuddered. 'They attacked you?'

'It was more like they were just ... goading me. Pushing me around. Trying to ...' Tom broke off, looked into her eyes. 'Trying to make me change.'

'And they got what they wanted,' Kate muttered.

'You think they *knew* you were lupine?'

He nodded. 'They had badges on their jackets – silver wolf's heads …' He clutched the overcoat tightly about him. 'Anyhow, I took them by surprise. Leaped past them before they could stop me.'

'Look, are you going to say hello to me or what, you rude little sod?' called Blood impatiently.

Tom turned to Blood and forced a weak grin. 'You made it.' He reached out his hand, and Blood shook it firmly. 'Better late than never, huh?'

'Late?' Blood frowned, opening the Merc's rear door for them. 'If anyone's late, *you* are.'

'We waited for you to show for hours!' Kate protested, as she and Tom got gratefully inside.

In truth, they'd been waiting for weeks, since they'd first arrived here in Chicago. It had been Blood who'd informed them he'd heard some big lupine event was being planned in the city. He'd warned them to stay well away – he'd certainly intended to. But Kate and Tom had known that if there was an opportunity here to scupper the lupine community's quest for power then it had to be taken. And a few days ago, to their relief, Blood had emailed to say he was going to join them after all …

'Those coded messages of yours are too much.' Blood scrambled into the driver's seat. 'I thought "21 Always Jealous WS" meant nine o'clock on the 21st between Evergreen Street and West Schiller.'

Kate shook her head. 'Nuh-uh. You got the nine o'clock and Evergreen bit right, but WS stood for Winter Solstice – that's the 22nd.'

'Today,' Tom said pointedly.

'Well, pardon me I'm sure,' grumbled Blood as he

started the car. 'Got worried sick when I couldn't find you last night. Been driving around looking for you pretty much ever since.'

Kate fluttered her eyelids. 'Nice to know you care.'

'Didn't know whether the 'wolves had got you, or the cops,' said Blood mildly, pulling away down the deserted street. 'I take it you're both still wanted for that double homicide in New Orleans?'

Tom nodded and grimaced. 'You were there. You know we're innocent.'

'You're the only one who can prove it,' Kate added. The three of them had survived a bloody showdown with Kate's mother, who'd killed two men, then later blamed it on Kate and Tom, making them dangerous fugitives in the eyes of the world.

'Who'd believe me if I told them?' Blood pointed out. 'I'd just be incriminating myself. Besides, I'm older than you two. They'd blame it all on me for corrupting you, stick me in prison or something.' His voice suddenly became terribly English and refined. 'And honestly, can you see me in one of those ghastly orange uniforms?'

Kate smiled. Blood was apt to slip into this voice; in his day job he worked selling upmarket real estate, and found the accent often impressed his customers. 'Let's just hope the police don't stop you now for driving with one headlight out,' she remarked.

'We'd better get well away from here,' said Blood, heading towards the highway. 'If Tom was seen in 'wolf form, he may have caused a stir. And if the police stop our car looking for witnesses ...'

'Good paranoid thinking,' Kate said.

'Thank you.'

Kate stared out of the window, willing herself to relax a little after her ordeal. She was no stranger to paranoia herself – nor to horror. Her whole family were pureblood werewolves, which meant that the lupine gene was in her – just waiting to be activated by mating with a lupine partner. Kate had railed against her lupine destiny. In the end, her parents had taken matters into their own hands: they'd abducted Tom and bitten him, turned him 'wolf, so he could turn *her*.

Luckily for Kate, things hadn't turned out as her parents had planned. Tom had been able to resist the lupine toxins. Though he'd succumbed and become 'wolf in the end, he was a *wereling* – a werewolf who retained enough humanity to temper the savage lupine nature. Together, he and Kate had escaped her family and gone on the run.

I should've stayed put, she thought miserably. *Should've stayed blissfully ignorant.* She'd always known the secret lupine community stretched clear across the United States, around the world even. But she'd never imagined that some of the 'wolves, tired of skulking in the shadows, were already plotting the day when they would come out into the light to run wild in the world of humans ... nor that her own, unbalanced mother would become one of their ringleaders.

'Well, whatever the circumstances,' Tom said from the back seat, his face angled to the hot-air blast of the rear heaters, 'it's good to see you, Blood.'

Blood nodded. 'I was hoping to see you less hairy, Tom. I take it you couldn't find Big Chief Medicine Man Jicaque, and his patented werewolf cure?'

'Oh, we found him all right,' Kate answered, a

touch sourly. 'In New York. And he could've healed Tom. He's healing other lupines there, right now.'

'So, what went wrong?' asked Blood.

'Nothing,' Tom replied. 'Except I realised that while we're still fighting the lupines, my own 'wolf might just come in useful ...'

'Well, I'm glad you've found a use for it,' Blood said dryly. 'But I imagine our friend Takapa has a good use for it too – stuffed and mounted on his wall, once he's taken you apart cell by cell.'

Kate shuddered and turned away at the mention of Takapa's name. It came from an old Navajo word meaning *Eaters of Men*. Somewhere out in the city's darkness, that evil albino freak was up to something. Takapa saw himself as the great saviour of the lupine race – utilising modern science in his quest to lead all werewolves into a glorious new age of freedom.

Freedom to hunt humans without fear of reprisal.

Freedom to kill and feed at will.

Maybe one day, the freedom to rule over all humankind.

It was a sick, twisted, impossible dream – and yet it seemed the 'wolves were beginning to believe it could come true. Takapa was undoubtedly a genius in his own freakish way; his genetic researches were stripping away the mysticism from the lupine condition, and while some 'wolves saw that as sacrilege, Takapa was determined to convince them it was a necessary step if werewolves were to survive in the modern world.

'We managed to sabotage Takapa's lupine army in New York,' Tom said, 'but so far, we've learned sweet nothing about what he's planning here in Chicago.'

Kate could hear the frustration in his voice.

'I may be able to shed some light on that,' said Blood.

Both Kate and Tom sat up straight in their seats.

'But first I'll tell you why I decided to join you in your little escapade,' Blood began. 'I was hanging out incognito in the Hamptons and was quite enjoying myself – until someone tried to kill me.' He sighed. 'By the size of his teeth, he must've been sent by your beloved mother, Kate. Perhaps because I *am* the only person who might be able to clear your names.'

Tom stared. 'What happened?'

'Much like you did tonight, I ran like bloody hell.' Blood shot them a glance in the rear-view. 'Then, having got my breath back, I decided it might be a little healthier to celebrate the festive season with friends.'

'And when *they* didn't want to know, you looked *us* up?' Tom asked dryly.

Blood grinned. 'Thought I'd take pity on my favourite urchins. Season of goodwill and all that.'

'What you're saying,' Kate interrupted, 'is that you've woken up to the fact that you'll never be safe anywhere until we end this whole nightmare for good.'

'What a ray of sunshine you are, Trolly,' sighed Blood. 'Still, if we're going out, we may as well go out in style. I've booked a suite at the Drake Hotel for the festive season. Would you care to join me?'

Kate smiled wryly at Tom. 'Gee, he really *is* Santa Claus.'

'The suite comes with an extra guest room.' Blood craned his neck around for a moment and winked at them. 'Twin beds only, I'm afraid.'

Kate's mouth went suddenly dry. She flushed when she realised Tom had gone as silent as she had.

'Twins is perfect,' Tom mumbled.

'Yeah,' Kate agreed faintly, resting her hot cheek against the cold glass of the window. Her green eyes gazed back at her from her ghostly reflection in the glass. 'Perfect.'

Blood took a sharp turn heading for Lake Shore Drive.

As he neared the intersection, Kate saw four men standing in the white glow of a streetlight. Dressed in black leather, they were almost one with the night, but she caught the glint of something shiny on the heavy jackets they wore. A shiver went through her. 'Slow down,' she told Blood.

Tom saw them too. 'Same guys,' he breathed.

Now Kate noticed each of the men wore a silver wolf's head pinned on his chest. The men stared back at Tom and Kate. One pulled out a cell phone.

'OK, let's get going,' Tom said. 'Like, now.'

'Make up your minds,' grumbled Blood, as he put his foot down.

CHAPTER TWO

They cruised through the thin traffic on Lake Shore Drive. The night was so black, Tom found it hard to see where lake ended and sky began; they mingled to form a long rumpled sheet of darkness behind the streetlamps. But as Blood left the highway and headed west into Uptown, the urban sprawl stole back some of the sky. There was still plenty of life around this part of Chicago in the small hours, beneath the twinkling fairy lights strung up above the streets: drunks mooching around the littered sidewalks, stray couples fumbling behind dumpsters, excited groups of young people spilling out of clubs, laughing and swaying, filled with festive cheer.

Merry Christmas. What a joke.

He wished more and more each day that he'd taken the cure when Jicaque had offered it to him. The old guru said you had to really *want* the cure to make it work, and Tom had been more concerned about the long-term view. He knew that he and Kate would only be safe if Takapa and Marcie Folan – Kate's murderous mother – were stopped for good.

A month ago, flushed with the victory over them in New York, Tom had felt that might just be possible. But now, after so many weeks cold and hungry, struggling to contain his 'wolf side when the moon was full or in times of stress and anger, he felt feeble and worn down. Yeah, right, like a couple of kids were ever going to take on the whole lupine community and win. Who did he think he was kidding? If he'd taken the cure, he'd be normal and he and Kate might actually stand a chance of …

… *of dying*, he realised, *torn apart by teeth and claws, helpless and screaming*. There was nowhere to hide, as Blood had discovered. There were too many 'wolves, too widespread. Tom knew they *had* to fight back – even if they died trying.

Tom suddenly saw they'd arrived. Kate had directed Blood to where their apartment squatted above a boarded-up deli, its two dark, square windows staring out blankly over the rest of the run-down block.

'Delightful,' Blood observed as he pulled up outside.

'It's somewhere to crash,' Tom said.

Blood gestured to the cracks and chasms in the brickwork. 'Looks like a juggernaut beat you to it.'

Kate opened the street-level door – Tom had agreed she would always carry the keys and what little money they had, in case he turned 'wolf and lost everything. He and Blood followed her up the damp wooden stairs to the first floor.

They reached the apartment's peeling door on the tatty communal landing. From the look on Blood's face Tom guessed he'd rather be standing barefoot in a nest of vipers.

'How do landlords get away with offloading slum rooms like this?' Blood demanded.

'By not asking awkward questions or for any

references,' Kate replied simply, as she worked the key into the lock.

'Is that a fact?' Blood cast a dubious eye over the door of the neighbouring apartment, which was in equal disrepair. 'How saintly of him.'

'Uh-huh,' Tom said. In truth, their landlord was a fat pig who owned a string of dingy diners. He had used them as slave labour, insisting they work long shifts washing dishes in lieu of rent. After that, going out 'wolf-hunting had been almost a pleasure.

Kate pushed open the squeaky door and led the way inside. 'Excuse the mess. We don't have many guests.'

'Good gods,' muttered Blood as he stepped into the room. He shook his head in horror. 'I don't blame you.'

Tom looked around the room and realised he'd grown used to the squalor. One big musty room served as bedroom, kitchen and living room. Kate's bed was a grubby mattress on the floor in one corner, while Tom made do with the sagging, moth-eaten couch. Thrift-store clothes were strewn over the threadbare grey carpet. Net curtains turned beige with age stuck to the condensation on the windows. A plywood screen hid the poky bathroom from view, but did little to keep out the gurgles of rusting waste-pipes and the stench of blocked drains.

'Pack your bags and let's get you out of this dump and into a hot bath,' said Blood grimly. 'Now!'

Kate grinned at him. 'Can I marry you?'

'Get in line, Trolly,' Blood replied. 'And Tom ... just get dressed.' Then he gestured to the home-made paper chains hanging from the stained, sagging ceiling. 'Nice touch, by the way. They really transform the place.'

'I want to be an interior designer when I grow up,' Kate said, equally deadpan. She had torn up an edition of the *Chicago Reader* to make the paper chains one night, in an attempt to cheer Tom up.

Tom hadn't had the heart to tell Kate how miserable the decorations made him feel. They reminded him of all the family Christmases he'd spent as a kid, warm and snug, stuffed full of food without a care in the world. His parents and Joe, his brother ... what kind of Christmas would they be spending this year? First they'd thought Tom was dead – and now, that he was a murderer ...

The thought of Mom spraying their old fake Christmas tree with pine air freshener like she always did when it came out of the attic, of Joe helping Dad roast the chestnuts and burning them black as usual ... all that soppy, sentimental crap that they did each Christmas, it made him want to cry and curse all at once.

He missed them so bad it hurt.

And the thought of them carrying on without him, however hard they might find it, left him feeling sick and hollow inside. It was like they were learning to forget him, to shut him out.

He hated the goddamned paper chains.

'Now then,' said Blood, his voice bulldozing through Tom's dark thoughts. 'While you two are clearing out of this hovel, I'll tell you what my contacts have told me about this pureblood gathering that's got the lupine world all whipped up.'

Tom turned his back to pull on a pair of boxers and some jeans beneath Blood's coat. 'We're listening.'

'First of all, Takapa, our favourite homicidal albino, is leasing a couple of properties here in Chicago –

including an industrial building on the West Side. He's been taking delivery there of some pretty high-tech laboratory equipment.'

Tom shrugged off the coat and searched self-consciously for a stick of deodorant. 'Sounds like he's up to his old tricks, messing with 'wolf genetics.'

'So what's new?' Kate said, shoving a bundle of underwear into a plastic bag while Tom conspicuously pretended not to notice.

'What's new is something very old,' replied Blood, producing a gilt-edged square of card from the pocket of his suit jacket with a flourish. 'I managed to procure this from a rather specialist burglar of my acquaintance. He finds a 'wolf address, waits until full moon, to be sure they're out on the hunt, then burgles the place in peace.'

'Nice trick. It's got to beat washing dishes, anyway.' Kate plucked the card from Blood's outstretched fingers and began to read aloud. '"The Bane Gallery cordially invites you to a Private View of König Man, to be held on December 25th, 00:00 hrs".'

'Christmas Day?' Tom said in surprise.

'Lupines aren't real big on human holidays,' Kate replied. She read on. '"Having lain preserved for centuries in a peat bog outside of Gottenheim, Germany, König Man was recently discovered ..." blah, blah, blah ...' Kate arched her eyebrows. 'Sounds real fun.'

Tom pulled on a pale blue T-shirt and a grey hoodie. 'Why would the purebloods be so interested in some ancient stiff pulled from a swamp?'

'My guess is it's a coded summons of some kind,' said Blood. 'Might be nothing to do with a man or a bog whatsoever.'

'The invitation says that accommodation will be provided – at someplace called Brook Mansion,' Kate said.

'That's the other property Takapa is leasing,' Blood informed them. 'My realtor contact here tells me it's a *very* nice place. It seems Takapa is determined to impress. Brook Mansion was set up as a luxury hotel, but the owners went bankrupt. Takapa started leasing it three months ago. As far as my contact knows it's standing empty.' He nodded at the invitation. 'In anticipation of this gathering, I imagine.'

'At least we have some proper leads now,' Tom said.

'What about the mysterious Sunday – the local who's been posting in the chat room?' asked Blood, taking back the card.

Kate screwed up her nose. 'Don't talk to us about Sunday.'

Tom nodded bitterly. 'We've arranged to meet up with him four times this month, and he's blown us out every time. He's got to be a phoney.' Tom paraphrased one of the posts in a high-pitched whiny voice. '"My dad's been abducted by 'wolves – they're forcing him to do weird experiments, and now Takapa wants to kill me. Please, will somebody help ..."'

Kate nodded, stuffed the plastic bag in her rucksack and flung some more clothes in after it. 'I reckon it's a 'wolf feeding a line to the likes of us and seeing who bites – so *they* can bite back.'

'Well, I'm not so sure,' said Blood. 'I had altogether too much time on my hands hiding out in the Hamptons, so when I read Sunday's postings I did a trawl through Chicago missing persons reports.'

Tom nodded. 'And?'

'Well, all your usual reports of punk kids and street trash gone astray, of course, but ...' Blood paused impressively. 'Also missing are three quite eminent scientists. All in the last six months, and *one* just before Sunday started posting – a guy called John Walker.'

As he spoke, a screech of brakes sounded in the quiet street outside.

Tom cast a nervous glance at Blood and Kate and crossed to the window. He twitched the nicotine-stained nets a fraction to peep through.

At first the street seemed still, with nothing to see through the flurry of flakes but the snow-drifted roofs of the endless low-rises stretching away into the night. Then he saw something; a big, red car parked across the street, the only one aside from Blood's that wasn't sporting a glittering white carpet of snow on its roof. Three or four guys were huddled inside.

'Shit,' he breathed, as Kate came to join him. 'I think we've been followed here.'

'Not hard to spot a Merc in this neighbourhood, I suppose,' said Blood, rubbing his hands together briskly. 'OK – you've officially finished packing. Let's get out of here.'

'Too late,' Tom murmured, feeling the all-too familiar nag of fear in the pit of his stomach. The driver's door had swung open and a tall Asian guy dressed in black leather emerged. Three other men – one black, two white – gathered behind him. Their silver wolf's head badges glinted brightly in the moonlight.

The Asian guy looked straight up at the window, scowling like he could see Tom and Kate through the filthy curtains. For a moment, a lupine glint of yellow showed in his dark eyes. The other men followed him, dark and silent as shadows, over to the street-level door that led up to the apartment.

'They're coming,' Kate said, her voice hollow, stalking over to the mattress to gather her things. 'And they're 'wolf.'

Blood looked at Tom expectantly. 'So you've got an escape route worked out, right? In case any howling heavies come to call?'

'Bathroom window,' Tom said. He swung his rucksack on to his back and slung open the bathroom's flimsy plywood door. 'It'll be a tight fit but ...'

He stuck his head through the small window – and saw a dark shape shift in the shadows below. 'No go,' he reported grimly. 'They've got it covered.'

A banging noise started up downstairs.

Kate ran a hand distractedly through her dark hennaed hair. 'That door wouldn't keep out a determined hamster.'

'Time for Plan B, then,' ventured Blood.

He led the way out on to the landing. Tom and Kate followed. The hammering from outside echoed frighteningly up the stairs.

Blood pulled a face. 'Bollocks. No place to hide. Looks like we're shafted, kids.'

Kate frowned. '*That's* Plan B?'

'Screw that,' Tom muttered. He crossed the landing to the neighbouring apartment and took a savage kick at the door – then swore loudly. It felt like he'd broken every bone in his foot, and the door remained shut.

Kate gave a high, almost hysterical laugh. 'Last action hero.' She kicked the door herself but with no more success.

'Allow me,' said Blood, and shoulder-charged the door. With a terrific, splintering crash it burst open.

'Just so you know,' gasped Blood, clutching his arm. 'That noise wasn't the door, it was my sodding shoulder.'

Tom shoved Kate ahead of him into the dark room. They'd never heard a sound from their neighbours in all the weeks they'd been here, and as his eyes grew accustomed to the dark, Tom realised why. The place seemed entirely empty save for dust and must.

With a still louder smash of wood and glass, the door downstairs finally gave way.

'You realise we could be thrown out of the local Neighbourhood Watch scheme for this?' muttered Blood as he tried to swing the splintered door back shut. But the latch was smashed and the door would not stay closed.

'We need something to push up against this door!' Tom hissed desperately, as heavy footsteps started crashing up the stairs. 'Or they'll just breeze in here and grab us!'

CHAPTER THREE

For a sick moment, as their pursuers thundered up the stairs, Tom thought they were dead meat. But then a banging started up at the door to their abandoned apartment. The men thought they were still inside.

'We're losing patience with you two!' snarled one of them. 'No one runs from us. Open up!'

Tom gave him the finger through the wall. 'Bite me,' he mouthed.

'You really think he needs an invitation?' enquired Blood acidly.

Kate stole across to the window, which overlooked the next street. 'We can reach the fire escape from the balcony,' she said.

Leaving the intruders banging loudly on the wrong door, Blood led the way out through the window. The rotting balcony, slippery with a thin dusting of snow, groaned under his weight as he clambered across it to the rusting rungs and railings of the fire escape that zigzagged down into the darkness.

Kate went next. 'Let's hope they don't have someone waiting on this side of the building as well,' she breathed, as she gripped hold of the icy cold railings and started to climb down.

There was a muffled thud and smash from their

apartment, and then a bellow of anger.

'Move!' Tom hissed, swinging his leg over the side of the balcony. The rotten wood split and gave way beneath him.

With a shout he fell forwards, reached out blindly for the fire escape, and caught hold of a slippery, rusty railing. He hung there, too shocked even to feel afraid as he dangled over the blackness beneath him.

'They must be in here!' came an angry shout from the landing, and this time it sounded like the door to the empty apartment had been knocked clear off its hinges.

'Drop down, Tom!' hissed Blood from somewhere beneath him. 'There's a bush, it'll break your fall!'

A second later Tom was crashing through sharp, wet foliage. His skin stung with scratches as he tumbled and fell, finally landing heavily on his back – or rather, on his well-stuffed rucksack. It had probably saved him from splitting his skull open on the frozen ground.

He lay stunned for a few moments. Then Kate and Blood appeared beside him and dragged him to his feet.

'Are you all right?' Kate asked, breathless from the descent.

'Think so,' Tom replied, feeling the scratches on his face.

'Had to sodding show off, didn't you,' said Blood. 'Come on, round to the front. We need to get to the car!'

Tom set off unsteadily after them, then heard an angry shout.

'Hey, wolf boy!'

He turned to see the Asian guy staring down from

the window above, flanked by two of his buddies.

'We know what you are,' the guy shouted. 'You can't run from us, man.'

'Watch me, asshole!' Tom yelled back.

'Mess with the Dark Chapter and you're meat, kid. We make the rules here.'

A shadowy figure loomed out from nowhere. Tom guessed it must be the guy who'd been watching the bathroom window. Tom tried to run but skidded on the icy ground, his momentum carrying him crashing into the guy, who was knocked flying.

Scrambling back up, Tom made it out into the street. With a squeal of tyres, Blood's Merc was suddenly reversing towards him.

'Get in!' Kate shouted as the rear door swung open.

Tom dived in beside her, Blood crunched the gearshift into first and the car tore away again. As they swerved past the apartment Tom saw more dark figures emerging from the crumbling building. He felt Kate's icy hand wriggle into his own.

Sirens were starting to sound in the distance. 'So, net-heads,' Tom panted, dabbing at his bloody face with numb fingers. 'In your dark and spooky chat rooms, have you ever heard of a group called the Dark Chapter?'

'Don't think so,' Kate said.

'Who the hell are they?' asked Blood.

Tom sank back into the rear seat and closed his eyes. 'I think we're going to find out.'

It was crazy, but Kate found her bed at the Drake Hotel almost *too* comfortable after what she'd been used to this last month. Though she was totally exhausted, sleep refused to come, no matter how much she tossed and turned.

She pushed back the covers and lay curled up on her side in her underwear and cotton T-shirt, listening to Tom's soft, rhythmic breathing in the bed across the room.

OK, so they'd cheated death one more time. But how much longer could their luck last?

What if Tom wound up dead before she could tell him how she felt about him?

'Jeez, I'm a complete soap opera,' she sighed to herself.

'Kate?'

Tom's voice made her jump although he'd spoken softly. 'Yeah?' she responded. She started to turn, then froze as she heard him getting out of his bed and padding across the room towards her. 'Tom?'

'Quiet,' he whispered.

A wave of heat crashed through her whole body as she realised he was getting into her bed. 'Tom, what are you—?' Her voice cracked as one of Tom's arms snaked under her neck, while the other curled around her waist, pulling her close to him. She shivered as he pressed his lips against her throat. They both knew damn well what he was doing.

'We shouldn't ...' she whispered. But it was futile. Her arms were already slipping around his smooth bare back, her fingernails grazing softly against his warm skin. She heard his breathing grow huskier. 'We can't ...'

Suddenly, Kate felt coarse hair bristling against her flesh. Claws raking against her skin. She opened her mouth to cry out but Tom's writhing body crushed the air from her chest, pinning her to the bed. She could feel her own latent 'wolf-spirit – that dark potential she'd sensed only in her worst nightmares – answer the call of his sweat, his saliva, his hands on her body. His claws pressed harder, puncturing her skin, and she laughed at the sweetness of it as the blood started to pour and pour …

She awoke with a choking scream, her bedclothes drenched with sweat.

'Kate?'

Tom's voice sounded urgent and concerned.

'Keep away from me!' she hissed.

'I'm right over here!' he protested from his bed across the room. 'You must've had a bad dream.'

'I guess I must've,' she said, clutching the bedcovers close to her. 'Sorry.'

''S'all right. I haven't had a great night myself.' He paused. 'What was it about?'

'Nothing. Forget it.'

'Uh … would a hug maybe help?'

'Just go to sleep,' she snapped, pulling the blankets right up to her neck, trying not to shake. 'I'm fine.'

'God, you can really wolf it down, can't you?' observed Blood at breakfast. 'No pun intended.'

Tom gave him a brief glare but decided he couldn't really get mad at the man who had snatched them from the breadline and placed them in the lap of luxury. It was only seven o'clock, but hunger was winning out over tiredness.

'I don't think I've ever seen so much food!' he said cheerfully through a mouthful of bacon, fried eggs, pancakes and syrup.

30

Kate was pushing a forkful of scrambled egg sullenly around her plate. She looked pale and drawn, Tom thought, and was clearly scraping the bottom of her laundry basket with an old thrift-store T-shirt that screamed 'Make-Out Junkie' in red letters. Maybe that was why she looked so uncomfortable this morning.

'Right then,' announced Blood, glancing around the vast, opulent breakfast room to check they weren't being overheard. 'We've lived to see another day, so let's decide what to do with it. We need a plan of attack.'

'Maybe we should start by checking out the Bane Gallery,' Kate said without much enthusiasm. 'See what we can find out about this private viewing of the peat bog man.'

'Good idea, Trolly,' said Blood approvingly.

'And if we're going to try to stop whatever Takapa's planning for Christmas Day, we should check out this industrial building you said he's got,' Tom suggested.

Blood nodded. 'I've got the address written down somewhere ...' He searched his wallet and passed Tom a piece of paper.

Kate put down her fork. 'Maybe *you* should go check out the building, Tom. I'll go with Blood to the gallery.'

'OK. Fine,' Tom agreed, a little surprised.

'I was thinking of going to the Bane Gallery alone, actually,' said Blood. 'If there are 'wolves there, you'll be more of a target than—'

'I want to go, OK?' Kate insisted.

Blood made a face at Tom. 'Knows her own mind, doesn't she?'

'Guess she does.' Tom felt himself turning red. 'Well, no time like the present,' he said, pushing his plate away. 'I'd better get going.'

'You'll need some cash for the subway, I suppose,' said Blood, removing his wallet from his jacket pocket.

'Round here, they call it the El,' Tom informed him.

'Do they? Bloody 'ell.' Blood chortled as he handed Tom twenty bucks.

Tom pocketed the cash. 'After that joke I feel better about taking this. See you both back here later?'

'By two o'clock,' suggested Blood. 'If one party hasn't returned by then, the others can come looking. After a bit of lunch, obviously.'

'Obviously.' Tom held up his hand in parting. 'See you, then.'

'Take care,' Kate said quietly. She didn't look up from her uneaten breakfast.

Tom took the El and rode the green line to Ashland out in the stolid urban sweep of the West Side. The clean, cold metal shell of the train carriage rocked him to and fro. Through the window the glass and metal skyline caught the sunlight and reflected it at onlookers in coruscating bursts. The sky was a beautiful shade of deep uninterrupted blue, and beneath it the pristine snow covering cars and sidewalks was slowly melting to mush.

As the El kept up its steady progress, fellow passengers jostling on and off at each stop, the whole sprawling, brawling city seemed just a little more carefree.

It would be so good to feel a part of that world,

thought Tom, stomach starting to churn at the thought of what could lie in store for him this bright, crisp morning.

Emerging from his station on to the street, Tom pulled on his woollen hat and buttoned up his denim jacket. Then he found the street he needed on the fold-out city map he'd grabbed from the Drake's lobby.

The landscape seemed to grow drearier the further west he walked. Tom kept his eyes down on the side-walk, hoping he wouldn't stand out; he knew there were some nasty neighbourhoods on the West Side. Then again, he doubted they came much nastier than the one he was headed for. Big cliché though it was, Tom couldn't shake off the feeling that he was being watched.

For about the hundredth time, his thoughts turned to Kate. She'd seemed so distant this morning. More than three months had passed since their lives had been flung together. He'd thought at first he had some passing crush on her, his emotions intensified by the extremes they were living through. But the feeling had only gotten stronger. He was totally crazy about her – but how could she possibly think of him as boyfriend material with all this shit going on around them?

He knew that he couldn't tell her how he felt until the 'wolf had been driven out of him for good. But with a sinking feeling, he wondered if she'd already guessed. Maybe she was pissed at him for even wondering if she might be interested in him in that way. Maybe that was why she'd been so aloof today, hold-ing herself out of reach.

Finally, his feet stiff and cold inside his snow-damp

tennis shoes – about the only footwear he had left – Tom turned left on to some nondescript street and saw he'd arrived at his destination.

He trudged past, head down, shoulders hunched, casting furtive glances at the building. At first sight it was just a three-storey pile of mouldering red brick, interspersed with squares of glass so caked with filth they failed to catch the slightest sunlight. Then he saw that the ground floor was very different – it had clearly been restored, the windows fitted with thick reflective glass. Etched on a tasteful metal sign was the legend UNITED LABORATORIES. As if in apology for the shabby state of the rest of the property, a builders' sign pinned above announced that redevelopment work was in progress. Tom shuddered to imagine just what kind of redevelopment was taking place within.

He sniffed the air. Though not in his lupine form, his senses remained heightened. An acrid, invisible pall of chemicals had settled over the warehouse like a shroud, but beneath it he could faintly detect human sweat mingled with the familiar musky scent of 'wolf.

He discreetly skirted the building, looking for a way inside. A high chain-link fence marked its perimeter and surrounded a large yard at the rear. In amongst the slushy tyre treads and footprints leading up to the yard, Tom saw what looked to be great, heavy paw prints. 'Bit of a giveaway,' he muttered under his breath.

The fence was rusting and in bad repair, but Tom could scent sentries guarding the obvious entrances and exits. Perhaps his best bet was to try and enter from above – the neighbouring warehouse was taller, and it looked abandoned. If he could get up on to the roof ...

The main door of the warehouse was stiff but not locked, and Tom was able to force it open quite easily. He found himself in a cavernous storage bay. It was dank and stank of urine and old, musty fabrics, despite the chill breeze blowing through the cracked windows. Rolls of carpet as long as a train car lay abandoned in rotting stacks.

There were no signs of life, but again, Tom felt he was being watched. His nostrils twitched as he caught the faintest trace of leather somewhere outside. 'Mess with the Dark Chapter and you're meat, kid,' he reminded himself somberly. He sighed. 'Let's see how far I can get.'

The elevator was dead, so Tom started climbing the mouldering concrete steps, heading for the roof.

As Blood drove steadily through the thick traffic to the River North gallery area, Kate pretended to be asleep so she wouldn't have to talk to him. Kind of mean, considering he'd just blown almost two hundred dollars on her in Banana Republic as part of his plan to gain them entry to the Bane Gallery ... but she just needed some time alone with her thoughts. She was feeling bad about insisting that Tom go off on his own. What if something happened to him, and she never saw him again?

If she was honest, she knew that he was the reason why she felt so screwed up right now. She wasn't used to all this weird emotional stuff. Her dream last night had left her starkly aware that her life was completely out of control, and her first instinct had been to shut down, cringe away from all this messiness. Be self-contained like she used to be, isolated in her bedroom back home, living through the Internet and shutting out the horror of her lupine family and their bloody, nocturnal outings.

The thing was, though, some stupid, reckless part of her knew that what she was feeling right now ... what she and Tom were going through together, despite all the fear and the uncertainty ... it made her feel alive. *Really* alive. Why couldn't she just give up to it? It wasn't like she couldn't *kiss* Tom. There was so much they could do without going all the way ...

But then, with him being 'wolf, with her own lupine genes designed to respond to him – she couldn't risk letting herself go with Tom until the 'wolf was gone from him. And by then, would he even be interested?

Would she even stay alive long enough to find out?

Jeez, life sucked.

'All right, Trolly,' said Blood, 'you can pretend to wake up now.'

Kate opened a guilty eye and found Blood was somehow cramming the car into a tiny parking space in a leafy avenue. She checked the address on the invitation, ignoring his remark. 'This is the Bane Gallery? Didn't take us long to get here.'

He looked at her thoughtfully. 'Lots on your mind, eh?'

Kate shrugged. 'I guess.'

'Want to talk about it?'

'No.'

'Thank bloody Christ for that,' said Blood, pretending to wipe his brow. 'Felt I should offer, but I'm reliably informed that I'm crap at being a shoulder to cry on.'

Kate smiled. 'Surely not?'

'No patience with whingers, you see,' he said, killing the engine. 'Pee or get off the pot – that's what I say. If you want something bad enough, go and get it, whatever it takes. And then, if you find you don't want it after all ... well, nothing's undoable.' He opened the car door and got out. 'Just walk away.'

'I'm so glad we had this little heart to heart,' Kate said wryly. She slipped the invitation back in her purse and climbed out of the car after him.

Blood wedged a handful of change into the parking meter and surveyed the building in front of them. 'As for when you're faced with something you *don't* want to do, running like hell would typically be a good plan.' He sighed. 'So why am I still standing here?'

Kate grinned. 'How do I look?' She opened her long black coat to show off her grey fitted trouser suit.

Blood made no attempt to disguise where his eyes were lingering, and when he finally spoke again, it was in the upper-class English accent he used for business. 'I think you look like every top realtor's dream assistant. Now, just follow my lead.'

Together, suited and booted, they walked up the steps to the smart gallery. With a shudder, Kate wondered just what they would find waiting for them inside.

CHAPTER FOUR

There was a chain on the door that led to the roof of the old carpet warehouse, but it was so old it had almost rusted clear away. A few well-aimed blows with a lump of concrete pulverised the links. Shoving the door open, Tom crept cautiously through it, back into the cold daylight.

What he found didn't please him. There had to be almost two metres between the warehouse and Takapa's building – and a dizzying drop down to the roof on the other side. You'd have to be out of your mind to try and jump it.

Or out of your body. Maybe if he turned 'wolf …

No.

Tom clenched his fists. He refused to rely on that side of him to solve his problems. He pushed out a deep breath. It got so tiring sometimes, fighting the craving to change – to feel that animal strength and power flow through his body …

He sprinted towards the edge of the roof, knowing he couldn't hesitate, couldn't doubt himself for a second – then leaped.

Suddenly he was plummeting through the air. He caught a glimpse of the quiet alley far below him as he swooped through the freezing air like a cut-price Spider-Man.

He landed badly. Pain tore through him as he crashed on to the concrete lip of the neighbouring roof, his fingers scrabbling through snow for something firm to hold on to. At last, he heaved himself over and to safety.

He stared up at the cold sky above, trembling all over, heart pounding and temples throbbing. He felt sick as he thought of the risk he'd just taken.

But he had made it. Point proved.

Whoopee.

He looked nervously around in case anyone had heard his clumsy landing and come to investigate. But the place remained deserted and silent.

Gingerly he stood up. One of his ankles hurt like hell. He flexed his foot. At least it wasn't broken.

He started to explore. Scraping the snow from a skylight, he peered through the grimy glass. It was just a storeroom, full of old bric-a-brac and clutter.

He was considering using it to gain entry, when a strange, creepy sound carried to him from nearby. Part chanting, part singing – like some weird uncanny choir were warming up their cold, low voices.

Tom limped over to the next skylight to investigate. He cleared the snow away with his stinging hands, then rubbed off the dirt caked underneath it. This window offered a very different view.

The shadowy room was lit by many candles. A blonde girl, wrapped in a crimson blanket, lay huddled, motionless, on the bare wooden floor. She looked about Tom's age. That creepy noise seemed to be coming from a group of sinister figures in the room, dressed in dark hooded robes. Tom listened, transfixed, as the strange guttural words, seemingly only half-formed, left their mouths and lingered in the smoky air. What the hell was going on? Was this something Takapa had organised, or just the way his followers got their kicks?

A stooped elderly-looking figure came into Tom's line of vision, also clad in a long dark robe – and clutching a curved knife in trembling hands. He began to intone another series of weird words and humming sounds, his voice booming with a depth and resonance that seemed at odds with his bent old frame. Even from up on the roof, Tom could sense the power emanating from him.

The girl started to twitch and jerk, like a puppet on invisible strings.

Tom felt his own heartbeat begin to jump erratically. The intonations seemed to echo and spin inside his head, making him drowsy. His eyes began to close ...

He shook himself awake – and saw that the girl was staring up at him. The old man was slowly advancing towards her, his knife outstretched. The girl's desperate eyes seemed to be pleading with Tom to help her.

Mind still buzzing, Tom yanked at the skylight, trying to open it. Whoever she was, he couldn't just stand by and watch this happen. It wouldn't budge.

The sinister chanting grew louder still, more discordant. It filled his head, burning his nerves.

Tom punched the skylight in frustration – and accidentally caught his knuckles on the metal frame. Pain scorched through him.

His gasp of shock turned into a slow howl of anguish as he felt his bones begin to burn white-hot. They began to lengthen, crack and re-form into lupine shape. The 'wolf-change had been triggered. Thick, dark hair sprouted from every follicle. It felt as though thousands of needles were pushing out through his skin. But as always, the agony was mixed with a delicious, heady exhilaration, impossible to deny. Now in its addictive thrall, Tom found it hard to remember his reasons for resistance. The world seemed real again, filled with stink and colour.

He drooled blood as his gums were ripped open by the extending of sharp, curving teeth. His fingers grew thick and stubby; dagger-like claws extended from his bleeding nails. His tennis shoes split apart as his feet widened and thickened into monstrous paws.

The transformation complete, Tom reared up and brought his front paws crashing down on the skylight. The dirty glass shattered into a thousand shards. Tom lowered his hulking form through the frame and dropped down to the chalk-scrawled floor.

The hooded figures jumped back in alarm, but the old man with the knife remained still, his head cocked to one side, listening. Tom realised the man was blind. Seizing the advantage, Tom rammed into him, sending the knife clattering to the floor.

There were shocked gasps and angry shouts from the other hooded figures. Tom bared his teeth and roared at them, but undeterred, three of them rushed over to shield the old man, while the other two fled through a door, presumably to raise the alarm.

Like a corpse jerking to life, the girl screamed, a full-throated, agonised sound. Tom turned to her as she struggled free of the blanket. Beneath it she wore only a cropped white T-shirt and shorts. She smelled sweaty and musky, unwashed. Tom couldn't help but salivate at the sight of so much soft flesh on display, at the thought of sinking his teeth into her pale, fleshy arm ...

Sickened with himself, fighting against every instinct his 'wolf possessed, Tom backed away from her, threw back his head and roared in angry frustration.

She recoiled from him, then scrabbled to her feet. Her movements were jerky, like she didn't have full control of her body. Tom knew the feeling. Then she turned and fled through the open door.

Tom turned back to the old man, who had shaken off his protectors and was signalling to them to stay back. There was no fear in his stern, lined face, just as there was no colour in his rheumy old eyes. Tom's animal instincts sensed in him that same great, unsettling power he'd felt up on the roof.

He turned and bolted from the room, ignoring the dull throb from his injured ankle, and followed the ripe, delicious smell of the girl.

It led him to a heavy door at the end of an empty, blank-walled corridor marked 'Emergency Exit'. He slammed the door open and bounded into a dark stairwell. He didn't need to scent the air to know the girl had fled straight down the concrete steps.

He was about to follow when he heard a door being flung open on the next floor down. A clatter of running footsteps rose to an echoing crescendo. The sentries he'd scented earlier, coming for him, getting closer. He sensed their eagerness. They were ready to turn 'wolf themselves.

As the guards turned the corner of the stairwell, Tom pounced from the top step, claws bared, snarling out a terrifying warning.

He landed in their midst, taking them by surprise and sending them scattering. One of them pulled a gun on him. Tom swiped the weapon aside with his raking claws. Two more tried to grip hold of Tom's neck, but he shook himself free, slamming his attackers back against the damp walls.

Then he was away, bounding off down the steps four at a time, gathering speed and meeting no more opposition all the way down to the ground-floor stairwell. The fire door stood open, and a shrill alarm was ringing idiotically, pounding into Tom's sensitive lupine ears.

He shot out of the building into the overgrown yard. There was the tall chain-link fence ahead; but a rusted corner of the mesh had torn loose from one of the concrete posts, enough for someone to slip through. The girl's scent led here; she'd got away, then, into the cold, quiet street.

Tom pushed through the gap and set off in pursuit.

He tried to force himself to change back into his human shape, but the lupine in him resisted – wanted to hunt down the girl and tear her sweet, delicious flesh into bloody chunks. Struggling so hard against the bloodlust that threatened to overwhelm him, Tom didn't notice someone jump out from the parked van until it was too late. He didn't see the hypodermic needle that was plunged down hard into his neck. He barely even felt the cold spill of its contents seeping through his powerful muscles, before a numbing red darkness smothered his senses.

Kate held her breath as Blood rapped smartly on the locked glass entrance doors of the Bane Gallery. She could see a security guard slumped behind the reception desk, shaking his head at them.

But Blood was not to be deterred, and kept up his banging with an occasional 'Hello there!'

Playing the uncomprehending Englishman in Armani finally got results. The guard, an enormous middle-aged man with thinning ginger hair and a collection of chins, lumbered over with a curious look in his eye. 'We're closed!' he called out through the glass.

'We have an appointment,' Blood called back cheerily. 'I'm from the realtors – we're here about the survey.' He showed the guard one of his Blood Lettings business cards, but Kate noticed he carefully covered the New Orleans address with his thumb. 'If you could just let us in?'

'Miss Black didn't say anything about appointments today,' the guard reported, shaking his head dubiously and setting his chins wobbling.

'An oversight, I'm sure,' Blood told the man confidently. 'I arranged the appointment with Miss Black myself. Look, do you think you could let us in while we sort this out? Dash it all, it really is parky out here.'

The guard's eyes glimmered with amusement at his exotic visitor. He turned to Kate. 'You English too?'

'Er – rather,' she said in a sort of high-pitched squawk.

Her answer seemed to please the guard. He unlocked the door and showed them inside. 'Where are you guys from? London?'

'That's very astute of you!' beamed Blood. 'Yes, indeed we are.'

'I love your accents,' said the guard, locking up

behind them then turning to Kate. 'Say something! Anything!'

She blushed. 'Er … one loves to play … croquet!' To her own ears, her strangulated screech sounded like she'd just sat down on a cactus in polite company.

The guard frowned.

'My assistant has a cold,' said Blood, shooting her a daggered look.

The guard, who seemed a little uncertain now, glanced back at his desk. 'Miss Black's up on the third floor – I'll go call her. Why'd you say you were here?'

'Valuation, old chap. The place needs a market value for the insurers, I don't doubt.' Blood grinned at the guard, eyes bright and twinkling. 'Tell you what, we'll head up to meet her while you tip her the wink we're coming. All right?'

'Well,' said the guard, 'I don't know if—'

'Jolly good!' called Blood, already heading for the stairs. 'See you later, then.'

Kate followed close behind him before the guard could say another word – and more importantly, before *she* had to.

'Nice going, Trolly,' muttered Blood in his more usual tones. 'You sounded like an Australian spinster on helium.'

'I never said I could do accents!' Kate protested.

'Just come on. If the mysterious Miss Black's on the third floor, let's check out the first and see how far we get.'

'And when that security guard finds out you're full of crap?'

'I play the stupid Englishman and tell him I thought this was the *Spain* Gallery on West Erie Street.'

Kate grimaced. 'And if Miss Black is a lupine and realises who we are?'

Blood shrugged. 'We run like bloody hell.'

At the top of the stairs they pushed through some teak double doors and found themselves in a spacious gallery area, all white walls and parquet flooring. Lengths of timber planking were piled in one corner, along with a collection of well-used carpentry tools. A few planks had already been laid out in a wide rectangle at the far end of the hall.

'Looks like they're building a stage,' Kate observed.

Blood mused on this. 'Maybe we've figured Takapa all wrong. Perhaps all he ever wanted to do was tap dance.'

Kate held up her hand. 'Shh …' She shivered as the hairs on the back of her neck pricked up.

Blood frowned. 'You all right?'

'I don't know …' Kate replied. 'It's just – just this weird feeling that there's something in here with us.'

'From that bulldog-licking-dung-off-a-nettle expression, I take it not a very nice something,' said Blood, looking around with studied cool. 'I don't see—'

'Through here,' Kate said, swallowing hard. She felt weirdly drawn to a matt white door set discreetly into one wall. Silently, she led the way over. Her hand froze as she reached for the door handle. A cold sweat broke out on her forehead. She was suddenly overcome by a wave of nausea.

'Trolly?'

'It's in there,' she whispered.

Blood sounded concerned now. 'Are you seriously telling me you're suddenly psychic?'

Kate pushed open the door. It opened on to a near-identical gallery, just a little smaller – and far chillier. Dozens of modern, uncomfortable-looking chairs were stacked in the centre in teetering piles. Towards the back of the room stood a screen fashioned from black, lacquered wood.

Blood surveyed the scene with a jaded eye. 'Well, either you were picking up the presence of a really rubbish art installation, or this is just a storage area.'

'What's behind the screen?' Kate asked nervously.

Blood crept stealthily over to the black screen then peeped behind it. Slowly, he straightened. 'You recall the invitation? Centuries-old König Man, dug up from a peat bog in Germany?'

'You thought it might be some kind of code,' Kate replied.

Blood turned back to Kate, his face grave. 'I'm afraid I was talking bollocks. He's right here.'

CHAPTER FIVE

Kate joined Blood by the screen to see for herself, and a frisson of deep, instinctive fear scratched down her spine.

The body, laid out on royal purple padding inside a glass casket, was a murky brown colour. Its form had been warped and twisted by the preserving sediment. The nose was little more than two holes poked into the ancient face; eyes were half-melted crusts, mouth fused into a barely discernible line. The arms were folded over the mutilated chest and stomach, and legs had shrivelled into awkward angles.

The thing was horrible, and to Kate it exuded evil. She shuddered, pushing her hands deep into her new coat's pockets, grateful for its warmth.

'For the attention of Araminta Black ...' Blood had picked up a hefty sheaf of papers that had been left on the glass case. 'Aha. Maybe we'll find some clues in here. This feller's König Man, all right,' he confirmed, flicking through the document. 'And this would seem to be the babysitter's handbook, prepared by the German labs – guidelines on proper storage, temperature requirements ... and a summary of the body's condition.'

'Disgusting?' Kate suggested.

'Goes into a little more detail,' said Blood, peering

at the page. 'This man did not die of natural causes. He was carefully tortured and executed.'

Blood read on, but Kate couldn't concentrate on his words. The desiccated eyes seemed to burn out at her from the misshapen face, and something dark inside her seemed to shift and stir. She recognised the feelings from last night's dreams – the feeling of the 'wolf in her blood, hungry for release. She bit her lip, backing away from the sinister exhibit.

'We need to get out of here,' she croaked. 'Now. I can't explain how I knew that body was here, but—' Suddenly Blood lunged forwards and clamped his hand over her mouth. Her eyes widened indignantly but he shook his head.

'Heard something,' he whispered.

Kate held still. There was a slow regular tapping noise coming from a distance away. But drawing closer. It sounded like it was being made by a formidable pair of heels.

Tom's senses drifted back to him one by one. It was dark; he could hear things shifting around him, whispers and scuffling sounds with a metallic edge. The ground was cold and hard against his back and butt, but perfectly smooth – he'd been propped up against something metal. His injured ankle felt a lot better – the faster metabolism of the 'wolf was a good healer.

An old blanket had been thrown over his naked body. Where was he? There was a nasty, chemical taste in the back of his mouth. He could smell the sweat of several men close by, and something sweeter – the girl he'd rescued. She was here too, somewhere in the darkness.

'He's coming round, Chung,' someone said.

'About time,' replied another voice.

Tom recognised it: the Asian guy he'd encountered the night before. Chung. He tried to speak back. 'You're from the Dark Chapter ...'

'Wolf boy's smarter than we thought,' said the first voice.

Again, there was the close, metallic echo – Tom guessed he was shut in somewhere small and enclosed.

'What did you do to me?' he asked.

'Knocked you out,' said Chung. 'Can't have you getting past us again, showing the whole damn neighbourhood you're a 'wolf. Chill out – the effects don't last long.'

'What do you want?' Tom persisted. 'Why did you come after me last night? Did Takapa send you?'

'Takapa? Get real. We don't take orders from him,' Chung replied dismissively. 'But now we know for sure you're a 'wolf, you're our business. We need to talk.'

Tom felt a brief wash of relief, but sensed he was still very much in danger. 'I know your Chapter's Dark and all, but can't we talk with the lights on?' He tried to sound nonchalant. 'Or is that against your religion?'

'Funny,' said Chung.

An emergency lantern clicked on, the kind Tom's dad carried in the car in case they broke down somewhere. Steady flashes of cold bright orange lit up Tom's surroundings, and he saw he was in the back of a van.

Chung was holding the lantern. He was in his early twenties maybe, with close-cropped black hair and a smooth complexion. He was flanked by three side-

50

kicks – one with a disconcerting squint, who stared at Tom with some hostility. Tom wondered if he was the guy he'd sent sprawling outside his old apartment. Behind them all, the girl from Takapa's building was lying still in one corner, apparently asleep, winking in and out of existence with the flashing of the torch. She was still clutching the crimson blanket tight about her.

'We don't have religion,' Chung said. 'We have *rules*. And if you're staying in our city, you'll do well to follow them.' He held out a hand. 'I'm Ryan Chung.' He gestured to the guy with the squint. 'This is Russ Fayn, my deputy and right-hand man. These two are Zac and Mike. They're my enforcers.'

Tom took the offered hand. Like Chung himself, Russ Fayn and the other two looked more like stock-brokers than hired muscle, despite the black leathers. Zac was a good-looking black guy with a carefully-crafted goatee. Mike was clean-shaven and prematurely bald.

'That's the thing with this city,' said Mike. Tom recognised him as the first man who'd spoken. 'Never know when you're going find trouble.' He dangled an empty hypodermic between finger and thumb.

'What exactly is it that you … *enforce*?' Tom enquired.

'We do what we have to,' said Zac, his voice soft and clear, 'to make sure no 'wolf in Chicago exceeds his kill quota.'

'Kill quota?' Tom echoed.

Chung nodded. 'The Dark Chapter keeps tabs on every lupine in the city – and who they kill. We've got people watching all over Chicago.'

'Doesn't take us long to find out about the latest

newbie in town,' Fayn remarked. 'You know how it is. 'Wolf can smell another 'wolf a mile away.'

'But something doesn't smell quite right about you,' added Chung. 'We needed to be sure.'

'Hence the fun and games last night,' Tom muttered.

'So – you gone hunting since you got here?' asked Mike. His voice was quiet but there was real menace there.

'No,' Tom said coldly.

Mike nodded. 'We thought not.' He clenched his fists. 'Otherwise we'd be doing the talking with these.'

Tom looked doubtful. 'I thought you tried to, last night.'

Chung crouched down in front of Tom, his almond eyes seeming to hold the amber light. 'Like I said, we just want to talk – and you to listen. We'll even over-look the trouble you've put us to in arranging this little get-together. It's just logic,' he said calmly. 'We're all 'wolves, right? We've all got to stay hidden. And if you want to live and hunt in Chicago ...'

'Five local humans each year,' added Fayn. 'That's your kill quota.'

'Exceed that,' said Mike, 'and we have to fillet you.'

Tom glared at Chung coldly. 'Five human kills?'

He nodded. 'We've calculated, any more than that, you risk exposing the 'wolf presence. We have an annual murder rate here of seven hundred. That can't be allowed to spiral out of control.'

Tom shook his head in disbelief. 'You're talking about killing innocent people, not balancing books! What gives you the right to dish out life and death by numbers?'

'My inheritance gives me the right!' said Chung fiercely. 'My pureblood ancestors came to Chicago in 1875, with the first Chinese immigrants. They had nothing but dreams of a better life in the land of the free. They formed the Chapter to help make sure they got it.'

'A better life for 'wolves in the land of the free *take-out*, you mean,' Tom retorted bitterly.

'The Chapter brought order,' argued Fayn. 'My family's pureblood too, came across from Ireland in 1920—'

'And why'd they come?' Chung broke in. 'Because they knew the Chapter was reining in those meat heads who figured they could just keep on killing and never get caught.' He turned to Tom, seeming puzzled. 'What gives with you, anyway? You sound like you're down on the 'wolf – but we've seen you change.'

'I'm a wereling,' Tom admitted. From the sudden looks passed between Chung and his buddies, he wished he'd kept his mouth shut.

'So ... no wonder you don't smell quite right.' Chung's thin lips twitched in a smile. 'You're that kid who's been causing old pink-eyes so much trouble.'

'I guess I am.' Tom looked Chung in the eye. 'Takapa's evil. He tried to turn New York into a battleground. And whatever he's up to here, you can bet it's going to be big, and it's going to be bad news – for 'wolves and humans alike.'

'So that's why you were spying on him, huh?' Chung's dark eyes held a trace of admiration. 'We trailed you to his place ... then we lost you for a while. What'd you find there? What's he's up to?'

'I don't know.' Tom shook his head. 'I got kind of distracted by the girl.'

Chung grinned as if in understanding. 'Well, it doesn't really matter anyhow; Takapa's acting all cute and kiss-ass to us. Guess he reckons he can buy the support of a pureblood Chung that way.'

'And a pureblood Fayn,' added his deputy, almost petulantly.

Chung nodded. 'In any case, so long as Takapa doesn't cause trouble, we'll leave him alone.'

'But he's invited a whole *load* of purebloods here,' Tom argued. 'What if they *all* fancy a little snack when they arrive, and go out on the hunt?'

Chung shook his head. 'The word's been put out – no one shows until Christmas Eve, and catering's being provided.'

'What does *that* mean?' Tom muttered darkly.

'Besides,' said Fayn, 'a lot of those pureblood families have their own Dark Chapters, in Philadelphia, Texas, Colorado ...'

'The guy's a harmless crank, if you ask me,' Mike put in.

'You,' Tom said, 'have got a shock coming.'

'And you,' said Chung, straightening up, 'have got five kills per calendar year, if you're planning to stay in town. Visitors of under a month get just the one.' He smiled coolly. 'Don't make out you're so shocked, wereling. We saw you chasing out there ...' He jerked a thumb at the girl in the corner.

In the next flash of sordid orange light Tom saw that the girl had opened her eyes. He stared at Chung, appalled. 'What?'

'You were chasing her. You wanted to make her

54

your kill.' Chung said it like it was the most obvious thing in the world.

Fayn smirked. 'She's not bad. Nice bit of flesh on her bones.'

'She was about to be knifed!' Tom snapped. 'I was trying to save her, not *eat* her.'

'You're something else, man,' said Zac. 'What are you, vegetarian or something?'

'Let her go,' Tom said simply.

'No,' Fayn objected. 'She knows all about us. She might talk to the cops, make trouble.'

Chung shook his head. 'We've got enough friends on the force. She wouldn't get anywhere.'

'I won't talk,' said the girl. She sat up, smoothing back her hair from her forehead. 'Takapa is holding my father somewhere. He'd kill him if I talked to anyone, I know it.'

Tom felt a tingle of realisation down his spine. 'Wait a second ... are you—?'

'My name's Sunday,' said the girl. 'Sunday Walker.'

As the heels tapped their way closer, Blood pulled Kate behind the screen that hid the grisly gallery exhibit from view.

Now some heavier footsteps could also be heard.

'Any sign of them?' A woman's voice close by, authoritative and clear.

'Uh, not yet.'

Kate recognised the security guard's voice.

'But they've gotta be around here somewhere, Miss Black.'

'We can't afford snoopers,' said the woman. 'Not when we're so close ...'

'They can't be snoopers,' said the guard defensively. 'The guy had a business card and everything. And they were English!'

'Just find them!' Miss Black snapped impatiently.

Kate heard the guard hurry away.

The door opened, and the heels tapped into the room. Kate held her breath, expecting them to make their way straight over to the screen. Then a cell phone trilled. For a terrible moment Kate thought it was Blood's, but it was Miss Black's.

'Araminta Black,' she answered crisply.

Peeping around the screen, Kate saw a reed-thin woman, businesslike in a well-cut black suit and red shirt. The heels were Manolo Blahniks. Her straight dark hair was cut into a severe jaw-skimming bob. She was maybe Blood's age, and her features were sharp and angular, save for her round, rather prominent brown eyes.

There was a light pause. 'Takapa? It's … it's good to hear from you. Is everything all right?'

Kate's heart thudded as she heard Takapa's name. And from the look on Araminta Black's face, everything clearly *wasn't* all right.

'An intruder? Was he apprehended?'

Kate looked at Blood. Were they talking about Tom?

'Well, I'm sure it's only a matter of time,' said Miss Black.

Blood gave Kate a reassuring wink.

'No, everything's well in hand over here.' Miss Black's brown eyes glanced shiftily about, and Kate shrank back behind the screen. 'Are your white wolves all set to leave the zoo tonight?' the woman asked.

Then she gave a forced, tinkling laugh, like someone pouring beads into a glass. 'Very well. Goodbye.'

Heels tapped closer and closer to the screen. They'd be discovered any moment.

Suddenly Blood nudged Kate, pointing to a stack of chairs to the side of the screen. Kate nodded.

She reached over and shoved the pile with all her strength. It toppled towards Araminta Black, who gave an almighty shriek and threw herself clear. The chairs crashed against the wooden floor with the noise of a small bomb blast.

Blood charged over to the door and flung it open. 'Come on, Trolly!' he yelled.

Kate was beside him in a flash. He led the way through the next gallery and back to the stairs – then skidded to a halt as he found the corpulent frame of the guard blocking their way. He was holding a policeman's baton like a club in both sweaty hands.

'Thank God you're here,' gasped Blood. 'There's been a terrible accident!'

The guard frowned. 'What?'

'You just fell over,' said Blood, shoulder-charging the man aside.

They didn't wait to see him crash to the floor, but the echoes of the impact were still resounding as they cleared the bottom of the stairs, slammed open the doors and fled back outside.

'*You're* Sunday ...' Tom stared at the girl in the slow orange strobe of the flashing emergency lantern. 'When you kept standing us up, we thought you were just some hoaxer, who—'

Chung placed a hand on his shoulder. 'Look,

wereling, you know the score now. Get out of here and take your pet girl with you. If she makes trouble for us – you're dead. We'll see to that.'

'I'm sure you're very efficient,' Tom replied coldly.

'Got to be,' said Chung.

Zac threw a pair of jeans and a black T-shirt at Tom's feet. Tom hastily turned his back to Sunday and pulled them on, then draped the blanket around his shoulders.

When he turned, Chung pressed a five-dollar bill into his hand. 'Nearest El stop's three blocks west,' he said. 'Racine. Catch you later – if we have to.' Then he opened the back doors of the van.

Tom's eyes were stung by the cold blue daylight waiting outside to surprise him as he stared out on to a deserted, snowy street.

Once he and Sunday were out of the van, the doors slammed closed. The vehicle started up and pulled smoothly away, leaving them shivering in the street, barefoot.

'Great,' Tom muttered. 'Our feet will have frozen off by the time we've found our way back.'

'Back where?' Sunday said bitterly. 'I've got nowhere to go. If I go back home, Takapa's 'wolves will be waiting for me.'

'Not a problem,' Tom told her. 'Me and Kate – Troll Lover to you – are staying with a friend at the Drake Hotel. Come back with us.'

Sunday looked away and began to arrange her crimson blanket into a kind of toga.

Tom couldn't help but stare at the collection of fine brown freckles littering the white skin of her arms. She still shivered so he passed her his blanket.

She took it gratefully and draped it around her shoulders. When she'd finished arranging her makeshift outfit, she looked at him in silence, clearly deliberating. 'Can I trust you?' she asked finally. 'Even though you're ... you know ...'

'I hope so,' he told her honestly.

Her face was grave. 'And ... and can you help me get my father back?'

'Why don't we talk about it on the El?' Tom suggested. 'If we freeze to death we'll be no good to anyone.'

Together, looking around nervously for any sign they were being followed, they began to walk quickly through the freezing slush.

CHAPTER SIX

It turned out people were so caught up in their panic of last-minute Christmas shopping that, beyond a few odd glances at two crazy kids going barefoot in this weather, no one paid Tom and Sunday much attention.

Amid the bustle, bags and chatter on the train, Tom quietly told Sunday a little of his and Kate's experiences, then listened carefully as she told her story.

'My dad's a geneticist,' she explained. 'You know the deal. Punching out defective genes in embryos, gene therapies ...'

Tom whistled. 'Clever stuff ... but kind of scary.'

'Not if you know what you're doing,' countered Sunday. 'And Dad does. Anyway, a year ago he started work at this new set-up – United Laboratories.'

Tom nodded grimly. 'Nice place. Shame about the owners.'

'He loved the work – loved the funding even more. Loads of theoretical stuff, a lot of it really wild ...' Anticipating Tom's next question, Sunday held up her hand. 'I don't know the details, but it floated Dad's boat,' she said. 'Then a few months ago, things began to change. He started looking tired. Getting jumpy. Bawling me out for nothing ... I snooped in his diary and found mentions of something called "Project Resurrection". Anyway, his moods got worse and worse. Then, one night – December 2nd – he never came home …'

Tom saw tears well up in her wide eyes. 'And you haven't heard from him since?' he asked gently.

'Nothing,' Sunday said hoarsely. 'I went to United Laboratories – but I didn't get past the security guard. He said he'd never heard of a Dr John Walker, and wouldn't let me in. So I went to the police and reported Dad as missing, but no one seemed too worried. A grown man, a doctor, not been seen for a few days? Probably just gone out of town with his colleagues for a conference or something, and forgotten to tell his daughter. I guess Dad's no kind of priority when there are young kids missing, out there all alone.'

'What about your mom?' Tom asked.

'There's just me and Dad,' said Sunday quietly. '*Was* just me and Dad. Anyway, since the cops wouldn't investigate, I thought I'd play detective myself. I checked through Dad's Internet history, called up all the web pages he'd viewed, to see if I could find some clue. And that's how I found out he'd done all this research into werewolves …'

'Guess that was kind of a shock, huh?' Tom murmured.

'Oh, it gets better,' Sunday assured him. 'The next day I got an anonymous note. It warned that if I made trouble trying to find my dad they'd find me, kill my dad in front of me and then tear me apart.' She paused, eyes glistening, too choked to continue for a while. 'I kind of figured they meant it. I couldn't be home alone so I stayed with friends … and started posting to that newsgroup for any info. I mean, what do I know about werewolves … in the 21st century!'

'I couldn't believe it either at first,' Tom said. 'Now I don't have much choice.'

'I'm sorry I couldn't meet you like we planned online,' said Sunday. 'Each time I went out it felt like someone was watching me. I got scared, backed out, didn't know who I could trust … Then one day, I guess I flipped. I was so sick of doing nothing … I tried breaking into United Laboratories to see if I could find out anything. I was caught, in like ten seconds – and that was that. I was so stupid …'

'Just what the hell were they doing to you in that room?' Tom asked quietly.

'From what I could gather, it was some kind of experiment – using a whole load of weird voodoo magic crap,' Sunday replied. 'I'd been there for four days. At least, I think that's how long. That guy … the creepy old blind guy … he kept coming to see me. Spoke stuff to me, weird words. Like a spell or something. They held me frozen, I couldn't move. He would bring in others, explain to them what he was doing like they were students, tell them how the words could control my body.'

'Words? You're sure they didn't give you drugs or something?'

'I swear. He paralysed different parts of me; stopped me speaking, stopped me swallowing – even slowed down my heart … like hypnosis or something.' She plucked distractedly at her crimson blanket. 'And then, when he and the others put on their creepy robes and all started chanting together, I'm telling you, Tom, it was like I was coming apart.

Like the whole of me was … unravelling.'

Tom shivered, remembering now how he'd felt as he'd observed the ritual through the skylight. 'How could anyone have that sort of control over someone just by speaking?' he asked.

Sunday shook her head. 'I didn't recognise the words. They were in some strange language,' she said quietly. 'But he told his students what some of them stood for. Chemical bases – thymine, guanine, cytosine and adenine.'

'And an order of fries to go,' Tom quipped, baffled.

Sunday glared at him. 'I know what those chemical bases are. Dad's worked with them throughout his career. They're the building blocks of DNA – and that old blind guy can build 'em up and knock 'em down just by opening his mouth.'

Kate got quite a shock when Tom let himself into Blood's suite at the Drake, a little before two p.m. Dressed in someone else's jeans and top, he was shivering with cold, and his feet had gone an awful blotchy blue colour. The curvy girl he'd brought back with him wasn't wearing a whole lot more …

'What the hell happened to you, Tom?' Kate asked. She flashed a tight smile at the girl. 'And who is this?'

Tom waved his arms like a stage magician presenting his glamorous assistant to the audience. '*This* … is Sunday.'

Kate stared in amazement.

'Damn,' said Blood. 'I was hoping she was a perk that came with the room.' He winked at Sunday and strode off to the bathroom. 'I'll fill the tub. A couple of hot baths are in order. Time for explanations later.'

'Thanks,' said Sunday gratefully. She looked at Kate. 'So you're Troll Lover?'

'Uh-huh.' Kate shook the girl's icy hand. 'And Sunday's your *real* name?'

Sunday forced a smile. 'My parents thought it was cute to name me after my birthday. But hey, I'm lucky. I could've been called Twelfth or March, right?'

Tom insisted Sunday jump in the bath first, and he settled for diving into his bed and burying himself under thick blankets. Then he filled in Kate and Blood on what had happened and all he'd learned.

Once Kate had heard what Sunday had been through, she decided to keep any future jealous twinges to herself. In turn, she and Blood told Tom about their findings at the Bane Gallery. 'Oh, and hey, guess what,' Kate added, 'I had an email from Stacy.'

Tom smiled. 'Yeah?' He and Kate had gotten to know Dr Stacy Stein while fighting the 'wolves in New York. She was a virologist in a Harlem hospital who'd developed what she'd thought was a serum to calm the bloodlust in lupines. But she hadn't banked on Takapa's agents perverting the formula so that the serum had stoked lupine aggression instead of soothing it. And the stuff had been made chronically addictive. Takapa had intended to use it to gain control over his lupine army. Luckily Jicaque, the old medicine man, was able to use his ancient wisdoms and powerful herbal techniques to swiftly break the addiction for most of the junkies, and then cure them of their lupine tendencies for good.

'I checked my email on Blood's laptop while I was waiting for you,' Kate explained.

'And on Blood's bloody bill,' added Blood pointedly.

Kate ignored him. 'Stacy's email said she's been keeping in touch with Jicaque, offering hospital beds for the homeless ones, helping them get into work programs, that kind of thing. *And* she said that Jicaque has learned something about what's going on here in Chicago. She wouldn't put it down in writing, but I've sent her Blood's cellphone number and told her to call.'

'Another sodding liberty,' sighed Blood with mock annoyance. 'There are some women who would kill for my private number, and you go handing it out to just anyone.'

'Marcie Folan would kill for it, I'm sure,' Tom said darkly.

Blood mused thoughtfully. 'Odd about her, isn't it? Since the two of you started running she's been proactive, to say the least, in hunting you down – or getting others to do so. And yet you've been in Chicago all this time and she hasn't bothered you once.'

Kate considered. 'I guess she doesn't know we're here.'

'Perhaps,' Blood concurred. 'Or perhaps something else has been keeping her and her psychotic friends busy. Something important.'

Tom looked uneasy. 'The upcoming show-and-tell for the purebloods?'

Blood nodded. 'And it's perfectly possible that it involves Sunday's missing father.'

'Do you think Sunday's dad is being held at Takapa's place?' Kate asked.

'Maybe,' Tom agreed.

'Unless the 'wolves have killed him already, of course,' said Blood quietly.

The bathroom door opened and Sunday padded out wearing one of the hotel's white towelling bathrobes. Kate found some clothes to lend to her while Tom took his turn to clean up.

Sunday's figure was fuller than Kate's. When Kate's spare pair of jeans wouldn't pull over her hips, she just grinned and declared that a pair of track pants she'd spotted might suit her better. 'So, you're staying with two cute guys at the Drake, huh?' she said lightly, brushing her hair in front of the mirror. 'Lucky you.'

Kate smiled. 'It's Adam Blood's room, really. Tom and I are his guests.'

'Are you two together?' asked Sunday as she rose from the mirror.

'We're just friends,' Kate replied, noting enviously the way her green sweater clung to Sunday's curves. 'That's all we can be.'

'Because he's, like, a werewolf?' asked Sunday. 'Or because—'

'Ask a lot of questions, don't you?' Kate interrupted sharply.

'Sorry.' Sunday shrugged. 'I guess I do. Dad always told me that asking questions was the only way to learn.' She trailed off, looking down at her feet.

Kate sighed. 'Hey, I'm the one who's sorry.' She slipped an arm around the girl's shoulders. 'I didn't mean to snap. I'm just kind of tense. Had a weird experience this morning.'

'Me too,' said Sunday with a shudder. 'What was yours?'

Kate found herself telling her tale for a second time.

She was trying to overshadow the unsettling memories of the corpse in the case by giving a particularly vivid description of the guard's fall on the polished parquet, when a shrill cellphone ring started tooting *God Save the Queen* in the next room.

'For you, Trolly,' Blood called. 'Some virologist or other …'

'Stacy!' Kate dashed from the bedroom into the spacious main living room and snatched the handset from him. She sprawled on a squashy cream leather sofa. 'Hey! How're things?'

'Been better.' Stacy's usually brash and upbeat voice sounded tired. 'I'm trying to arrange holiday cover so I can come visit you.'

'You're coming to Chicago?' Kate cried.

'Maybe. Jicaque insists we both need to be there.'

'Jicaque is coming too?' Kate felt excited but a little scared. 'Oh God. Things are way bad, right?'

'I don't know, Kate,' Stacy replied. 'All the old buzzard's said to me is, "Our beliefs are opposed, but as science and magic come together, so must we." In Chicago, of all places. Which is fine for the old hippy medicine man with no ties, but kind of tricky for the medicine woman with a stack of them.'

'Stacy … I don't mean to lay a guilt trip on you, but right now we need all the friends we can get,' Kate told her. 'And I know Jicaque's hot on magic, but it looks like Takapa's got some weird sciencey stuff going down too. Kidnapping scientists and God knows what else. If you were here, maybe you could help us work out why.'

'That's me. Stacy Stein, expert in weird sciencey stuff.' Kate heard her sigh loudly down the phone. 'I guess I can leave Jasmine looking after the kids on my programs, but I still need someone to cover my shifts ...'

Kate smiled. 'I'll bet you're a pro at emotional blackmail.'

'Takes one to know one,' replied Stacy. 'Look, I'll see what I can do, OK?'

'Sure. Well, when you get here we're good and easy to find – at the Drake Hotel in Streeterville.'

'How'd you swing that?' Stacy exclaimed.

Kate grinned. 'You know that guy who answered the phone ...?'

'Oh my God! He's rich!' cried Stacy. 'He sounds cute, too – is he British?'

Kate smiled over at Blood. 'He is – to both those comments. He reckons if you have to make a stand, you may as well do it on a deep-pile carpet.'

'Rich and cute. Screw this place, I'll be with you as soon as I can,' said Stacy, sounding just a little brighter. 'Bye-bye.'

Kate hung up and tossed the phone back to Blood.

He smiled rakishly. 'She's crazy about me already, isn't she?'

Before Kate could compose a suitably devastating put-down, Tom emerged from the bathroom, a white fluffy towel around his waist, face flushed by the hot bath, and hair ruffled and spiky. 'Was that Stacy?' he asked. 'What did she want?'

Sunday poked her head out from the bedroom. 'Who *is* Stacy, anyway?'

'Enough of the recaps,' Kate said briskly. 'Sunday, get in here. Tom, go get dressed. I think it's high time we all worked out what the hell we do next.'

She knew she sounded bossy but she didn't care. They needed to keep up the momentum. Because after what she'd seen this morning, Kate knew that time was running out, and that something truly malevolent was hatching in this freezing city.

'This is the mother of all long shots,' Tom sighed, as he and Blood braved the crowds filing out from Lincoln Park Zoo. The zoo was closed already, and the park would soon follow. Tom just hoped that his heightened senses would help him and Blood evade security and get inside.

'That stick insect Araminta at the gallery was very specific on the blower to Takapa,' Blood reminded him. 'She asked if his white wolves were ready to leave the zoo *tonight*, and it sounded to me like they were.'

'I know, I know, and there are two white wolves on loan to Lincoln Park,' Tom said. Kate had unearthed that little gem while flicking through the tourist information left in their room at the Drake. 'But Takapa stealing a couple of wolves just seems stupid.'

'Those wolves are incredibly rare, practically extinct outside of zoos,' said Blood. 'Maybe Takapa wants them stuffed as teddy bears, I don't know. The point is, they seem to figure in his plans somehow.'

'But white wolves could just be a codename for something,' Tom grumbled.

'Ah, yes, just like the König Man *wasn't*,' said Blood pointedly. 'Even if it *is* a codename, activity in the zoo tonight would seem a likely possibility, don't you think? With any luck we'll overhear or see something that might give us a clue to whatever it is they're planning.'

'Sounds like something the Dark Chapter should know about,' Tom observed.

'Maybe they already do,' said Blood sourly. 'Shame they're not listed in the phonebook, isn't it? We could have called to check. Meantime, stop your whingeing and use that supersnout of yours to help us dodge security.'

Tom nodded resignedly. Truth was, he'd rather have paired off with Kate and gone to check out Brook Mansion, the address promising accommodation on the invitation to the Private View. Chung had said the purebloods were due to arrive Christmas Eve – if they wanted to poke around for some clue as to what was going on, the sooner they moved the better.

Kate had insisted that Tom should go with Blood so that she could do some female bonding with Sunday – check she was fully legit. That made perfect sense, but he couldn't help feeling she was trying to avoid time alone with him.

Tom and Blood waited for an hour or so, flitting between hiding places in the park grounds. The musty smell of the zoo animals was deadening Tom's nostrils to the scent of any 'wolves that might be lurking. They tried scanning the snow for lupine tracks but the main pathways had been all but cleared by the tramping of visitors' feet.

Then Tom spotted a door ajar in an outbuilding near the zoo's entrance. 'Worth checking out?' he whispered.

Blood nodded. Silent as shadows, they swiftly crossed to it and sneaked inside. It was a small kitchen area for the staff.

'Sloppy security,' Tom observed.

Blood cleared his throat. 'Sloppier than you think. Seems we were too late in coming here.'

He pointed down at a puddle of blood slowly seeping from beneath the table.

Bracing himself, Tom stooped to find the mutilated body of a guard on the floor, huge claw marks scored in his uniform. 'He's still breathing,' Tom reported. 'We should get help.'

'Er, I second that suggestion,' murmured Blood, looking past him at the door they'd just come through.

Tom swung around to find the dark brown bulk of a massive werewolf framed in the doorway, its eyes gleaming like white gold. A thick stream of drool splashed down on to the tiled floor from its huge jaws. With a low growl it stalked menacingly towards them.

CHAPTER SEVEN

Kate and Sunday had gone to pick up Dr Walker's car from where Sunday had left it outside a friend's house in Bucktown. Night was starting to fall, but the streets were still busy. Festive carols floated out from cafés and bars, as well-heeled couples and groups of friends bustled about with bulging shopping bags, grabbing caffeine kicks and beers to help ease the Yuletide hassle.

To pass the time as they walked, Kate told Sunday something of her lupine upbringing. Sunday listened in silence, wearing an expression that sat somewhere between shock and sympathy. When Kate finished Sunday still said nothing. Then she gave Kate's fingers a squeeze, and the silence between them felt lighter.

Finally, on a quiet street lined with cars, Kate spotted one that stood out from the rest – it was still carpeted with snow, clearly left unused for some time.

Sunday produced an ignition key and pressed a button. The Chrysler's hazard lights fluttered brightly as the doors unlocked. She gestured for Kate to get in on the passenger side. 'There's a scraper under the seat. Pass it to me?'

Kate did so. She sat shivering in the cold car while Sunday scraped viciously at the thin ice on the windshield. When it was clear, Sunday clambered into the driver's side and started the engine. It growled into life first time. Freezing air spewed from the vents, and Kate swiftly turned the heater to its highest.

'Guess we should be going,' Sunday murmured.

'You don't want to stop in and say hi to your friend?' Kate asked. 'You've been missing for days – won't she be worried?'

'Don't think so.' Sunday shook her head. '*He* got kind of freaked out by me running around like a lunatic and babbling about werewolves. He didn't exactly tell me to hurry back soon.'

'Was he anyone special?'

'He had potential,' said Sunday, smiling sadly. 'Guys, huh? Can't live with them, can't tell them your dad's been abducted by mythical creatures with a grudge against humanity.'

As the car began to warm, Kate's nostrils twitched with a sweet, cloying scent.

'Cherry tobacco,' said Sunday softly. 'Dad's smell. Jeez, I miss him.'

'I miss mine, too,' Kate told her. 'Despite knowing what he is, and all that he's done ... how he stands by and lets my mom run wild no matter who gets hurt ... I hate him for it – but he's still my dad.' She looked away, her vision misting with tears. 'When I was a kid, I loved him so totally. So absolutely. I thought he was the strongest man in the world. But I know he doesn't believe in the dream my mom and Takapa are chasing. He's just too weak to stand up to them.'

'Maybe he just loves your mom,' shrugged Sunday. 'Loves her too much.'

'Loves her more than me,' Kate said. The words

tasted like puke in her mouth. 'Whatever. I still miss him.'

Sunday gave Kate's arm a light squeeze. 'I never knew my mom,' she said, starting up the car. 'She died when I was three. If something happens to Dad too, I ...' She looked at Kate. 'Life's so fragile, isn't it? You just kind of go through life thinking everything's cool, and that it's all for ever. But then ...'

'I know,' Kate said. 'But we'll find him, Sunday. We'll get him back.'

Sunday nodded, wiping her eyes with the back of her hand. 'OK. I'm cool. Here we go,' she said, nudging Kate's arm. 'Sunday driver on the loose.'

Kate smiled faintly as Sunday swung the big car out into the evening traffic.

They took the Eisenhower right to the end of the expressway, then Roosevelt Road out into the snaking side streets of exclusive Oak Brook. Kate looked out of the window, surveying the neighbourhood through the evening gloom. The huge houses were set so far back from the road behind walls, trees and railings that you could only glimpse their ornate glory. There were no sidewalks; Kate didn't imagine the residents walked anywhere, and they were too far from town or even the nearest mall for curious tourists to come looking. She imagined the fat cats of this neighbourhood reclining in leather armchairs in their sumptuous living rooms, or maybe looking out over their estate, at the Jags and Porsches and Mercedes sedans that poked their elegant noses out of multiple garages, entirely mindless of the world outside. Never dreaming that monsters had set up shop in their perfect neighbourhood.

'How's the navigation going, co-pilot?' prompted Sunday.

'Sorry,' said Kate, peering at the map. 'I think our turning is coming up. Third left.'

Once she'd taken the turn on to a snaking, leafy driveway, Sunday slowed the car. 'Maybe we should park here and go in on foot,' she said.

Kate agreed, and soon they were making their way by flashlight up the deserted drive. Five minutes later, large wrought-iron gates loomed ahead of them, fashioned with serpentine spirals. An impressive sign set into the high perimeter wall proclaimed the entrance to: BROOK MANSION – LUXURY ACCOMMODATION.

'Takapa's really pushing the boat out,' Kate observed.

'A flashy front to pull in the people he needs – while his real lair is a crumbling slum,' said Sunday sourly.

'But of course, the people he's aiming to impress won't see that,' Kate murmured. She peered through the gates, and listened hard for any sound of movement. 'It seems deserted, anyway,' she muttered. 'And there are no lights on in the building.' She took a deep breath. 'Let's try to get inside – climb over the gates.'

'What about security?' Sunday queried nervously. 'Alarms ...'

'This place is laid on for 'wolves, right?' Kate mused. 'A lupine is not going to be able to punch in security codes with a delicate paw, is it? It's just going to come skulking up, scale the wall and drop down out of sight. They wouldn't want alarms set off every time that happened. Burglar alarms sounding off might bring the police snooping around. Takapa wouldn't want that either.'

Kate looked up at the gate – then at Sunday. 'You don't have to come with me, you know,' she said quietly. 'I mean, if we meet someone – or some*thing*—'

'I need to know what happened to my dad,' said Sunday quietly. 'I'll risk it.'

Kate gave her a rueful smile. 'Then let's get going.'

Tom backed away as the massive 'wolf entered the zoo kitchen, its eyes narrowed, preparing to attack.

Blood dashed behind the heavy kitchen table. He shoved it forwards just as the 'wolf pounced, teeth bared. The table's sharp edge cracked into the beast's enormous jaw, stunning it for a second.

'Leg it!' Blood shouted. He pushed past the animal's bulk and raced out of the door.

Tom went to follow, skidded in the security guard's blood and fell on his butt. He pushed himself up, hands covered in gore. His gut twisted as his mouth began to water.

Senses reeling, he knew he had to get out, had to lead the 'wolf away from the wounded man. He ran blindly into the freezing night, scenting the air for Blood. But all he could smell was the blood on his palms.

Behind him he could hear the heavy footfalls of the angry 'wolf as it pelted after him.

Tom knew he didn't stand a chance on open ground. He jumped a low wall and started scaling the chain-link fence that stood behind it. He almost lost his grip on the wire as the lupine hurled its bulk into the fence, trying to bring him crashing back down to earth.

Gritting his teeth, Tom kept climbing. Heart pounding, he swung himself over the top of the fence and clung there, panting for breath, trying to collect his thoughts. But the smell of the blood was blotting out his other senses. He spat out a thick mouthful of drool and tried to wipe his bloody hands clean on his jacket.

His desperation made him careless. The 'wolf below slung itself against the fence with incredible force. The metal mesh jolted and shook, and Tom lost his tenuous foothold. He fell, and landed heavily on the other side, the breath knocked out of him.

The 'wolf snapped its jaws at him, teeth scraping at the wire links like it wanted to tear its way through to him. But then the sound of lupine howling carried to Tom's ears. It kept breaking off at odd intervals, as if Takapa's agents were signalling to each other – but saying what?

The 'wolf stopped snarling at him, turned and bolted into the shadows.

Tom breathed a shaky sigh of relief. But then there came a deeper, more savage growl from behind him.

He turned to find an enormous brown bear looming over him, its ivory teeth bared in ferocious warning.

As he shrank away from the animal's massive bulk, Tom knew there was no escape. The beast was enraged by the intrusion on its territory. Now, in the dim lighting of the enclosure, Tom saw it screw up its black eyes in hatred and flare its enormous nostrils. Roaring, slavering, it stretched its jaws wide open and lunged for him.

Desperately, Tom tried to roll clear of the great animal's reach. Too late. The hump of muscle on its shoulders rippled as its heavy paw swiped at Tom's shoulder, claws scraping his flesh and bruising him down to the bone. He shouted out, realised he was rolling down a concrete slope.

The cold water slapped into his face; it was like coming up against a brick wall. He'd fallen into the bear's bathing and drinking pool. Already the beast was hulking towards him.

Tom backed away further into the water. A jolt of fury flared through him.

A bear. What kind of sick joke was fate playing on him now? A goddamned bear had *started* all of this.

Back in Seattle, on holiday with his folks, Tom had gone bathing in a river and come up against a brown bear. It had scared him out into the rapids and he'd been swept away. He'd survived – only to be found by Kate's family, and bitten. Then the nightmare had really begun.

So now it was going to end as it had begun – with some stupid, freakin' bear? The poor innocent kid he'd been last summer hadn't stood a chance against a grizzly twice his size.

Things were different now …

As the bear waded into the water, ready to tear its quarry apart, Tom felt the 'wolf inside him storm out of the shadows. His body grew fever-hot. His chest expanded, sodden clothes tearing away. Bones popped and cracked like blazing wood. Muscle thickened on his every limb. Water churned about him as his limbs thrashed in the excitement of change.

The bear paused upright, sniffing the air, suddenly uncertain.

Metamorphosis complete, Tom lunged forward, heavy paws raking the bear's chest, knocking it backwards. They crashed down beneath the churning waters, where it was black as pitch. The bear gripped him tightly, hooking its claws into his back, tearing at the skin. Tom choked on water and blood, tore himself free of the bear's deadly embrace and swam for the side of the pool. The thrashing in the water told him the bear was close behind.

Tom turned, roaring as he swung a heavy paw into the bear's snout. He knocked the animal back into the water with an explosive splash.

This time when the bear surfaced it was on the other side of the pool, skulking away into the dim corner of the enclosure, its battle lost.

Tom growled at the retreating bear, fighting his instincts to chase after it and rip out its hairy throat. Then he heard the distant, ululating howls of the werewolf pack, signalling to each other once again. And this time, he caught a higher, more mournful note – the keening cry of a real wolf.

A dim memory shone through his clouded consciousness – this was important. This was why he had come. He remembered Adam Blood, and tried to zero in on his scent.

Nothing. Hopefully that meant Blood had got well away; he wouldn't stand a chance with the lupines on his own.

It was up to Tom.

He tore at the enclosure fence with his teeth until he had ripped a hole there large enough to push through. Then he was out in the zoo concourse, racing in the direction of the wolf cry. The heavy moon was nearly full and it lit the night like a dull lantern, lending him strength; he exulted in the power that coursed through his body. As he ran he breathed in the exotic scents of the beasts and birds around him, their food and fear, their muck.

Another howl sounded, much closer now, and Tom quickened his pace. Then something leaped out from the foliage lining the path, smashed into his side and knocked the breath from his body. Tom rolled over, righted himself – in time to see another 'wolf, slighter than the one he'd fled from but just as savage, bearing down on him. Its fangs gleamed in the yellow moonlight.

Tom kicked up his hind legs under his assailant and twisted his body around, propelling the attacking lupine through the air. It went tumbling over Tom's head and landed awkwardly on its back. Tom leaped to his feet before the other 'wolf could recover and pressed a paw down hard against its throat. The 'wolf struggled and writhed, but Tom kept up the chokehold. Finally, gasping for air, its muzzle flecked with thick white saliva, the creature closed its eyes and lay still.

Only now did Tom remove the pressure. The 'wolf did not stir, but began to breathe again in shallow gasps. They had been well matched in the fight; both about the same size and musculature. Both similar colourings, for that matter ...

Reckless with victory, Tom had a wild idea. He rubbed his body against that of the unconscious 'wolf, hoping to gain a little of its scent before it could revert to its human form. As an urgent howl went up from beyond the trees, he chased off in the direction of the sound.

A truck stood in the grounds, its engine idling.

Three lupines clustered around the rear doors that hung open like metal jaws. Inside, Tom realised, were the two white wolves. Their fear and confusion made a thick reek in the air – luckily for him.

As Tom approached, the other 'wolves jumped on board. They paid Tom no heed as he followed them into the cold, smelly maw of the van. One of the white wolves whined. The other snapped at its abductors, the fur on its back bristling. Both were cuffed roughly around the chops by a barrel-chested lupine; Tom realised that this was the 'wolf he and Blood had faced in the outhouse, and prayed nothing of his human scent now remained.

He heard the van doors slam. Then the engine roared and the vehicle jerked away.

CHAPTER EIGHT

In the end, Kate and Sunday found it remarkably easy to gain access to the grounds of Brook Mansion. Once they'd scraped their way over the fence, they stealthily made their way towards the dark, impressive shadow of the hotel building.

Suddenly, a security floodlight snapped on with stadium intensity. They threw themselves down to the freezing damp lawn.

'Stay still,' Kate hissed. 'Cats and owls and critters must set these things off all the time.'

There was no sign of anyone coming to investigate, and after a few minutes the floodlight switched back off.

By staying low, they kept clear of its sensors. Soon they were pressed up against the stonework of the hotel itself.

'Are you sure it won't be alarmed?' Sunday whispered.

'Like I said, I really doubt it,' Kate replied.

'And no one came looking when we triggered the floodlights,' murmured Sunday. She sighed softly. 'So, should we break a window?'

'Let's give it a try,' Kate agreed. 'And just hope that not everywhere is double glazed!'

After a good deal of nervous thumping with the flashlight, Kate neatly cracked in two a pane of glass beside the main doors. Working together, and with some careful manoeuvring, she and Sunday got the pieces cleanly free.

'After you,' suggested Sunday.

Kate wriggled through into the softly carpeted reception area. 'No alarms,' she reported. 'It's as quiet as the grave.'

'Nice,' murmured Sunday, coming through after her. She flicked on the flashlight, but its light was failing; the hotel's opulence revealed only in vague yellow pools.

'Typical,' Kate sighed. 'Let's get exploring before the light gives up all together ... try to find an office or something.'

There was nothing unusual on the ground floor, so they stole up the stairs to the first floor. Soon they stood in a grand-looking corridor, studded with dark oak doorways. The nearest door stood ajar, and Kate peered inside with the flashlight. It was a bedroom, with an en-suite bathroom, furnished expensively and stylishly in neutral colours. They tried the next few doors and found similar rooms.

'Should we steal some towels and call it a night?' quipped Sunday.

'There has to be *something* useful here,' Kate retorted.

After a cursory inspection of several more bedrooms – and what was presumably a conference room with chairs lined up in neat rows before a kind of lectern – they found an elegant stairway at the end of the corridor, leading to the second floor above.

Kate cautiously led the way. But as they reached the landing, she had an uneasy feeling in the pit of her stomach. The flashlight bulb was barely glowing by now. She shook it disconsolately. 'Pretty soon we're going to be completely in the dark.'

'Let's take a chance,' said Sunday. She found a light switch and flicked it on. A few moments later, the fluorescents set into the ceiling hummed into life, illuminating another hallway – but this time with just one heavy-looking oak door leading off it.

'The penthouse,' Kate declared.

Sunday pressed her ear to the door, her pretty face creased in concentration. 'I can't hear anything.'

'We'd have seen lights on if anyone was at home,' Kate reasoned. She pushed the useless flashlight into her jeans pocket and gripped the door handle. 'But get ready to run like hell if I'm wrong.'

She pushed the heavy door open.

It was dark inside, and a wave of humid warmth hit them – the temperature was far higher in this room. But nothing stirred in the darkness.

She groped inside for a light switch. Her fingers rustled against something and she almost cried out, before realising it was some kind of plant. Reaching higher, her hand closed at last on a thick cord, and she pulled downwards.

Dim lights flickered on in the high ceiling, revealing a long, incongruous room. The plant she'd brushed against was part of a broad strip of exotic flora that stretched right around the room's perimeter, covering the windows and framing three doors set into the far wall. A twisting narrow path led through a forest of bizarre items that filled the floor space: sinister sculptures in random places – with chairs positioned right up close, facing them; a fountain gushing over marble spheres, the cool gurgle of its water deliciously inviting in the stifling heat; to its side, a ball pool – like the kind at kids' activity centres. Odd, alien mobiles hung down from the ceiling on invisible wires, windchimes gently clinked together in the draft from the doorway.

'Takapa went for a different look up here, then,' Kate said wryly, staring around in amazement. She found herself thinking the chairs were placed far too close to each statue to allow a full visual appreciation. Then she realised that the chairs seemed to be positioned so that someone might sit and *touch* the sculptures. *Everything* in this room was about touch and sound.

With a sinking feeling, Kate realised she'd been wrong to assume that the place must be empty because the lights were off. She turned to Sunday. 'Whoever's staying up here must be blind.'

'Blind,' echoed Sunday softly.

Suddenly, Kate realised the girl was trembling. 'What's wrong?' she hissed.

'The old guy,' Sunday whispered, her blue eyes wide and frightened. 'The one who did that weird magic stuff to me at the warehouse. *He* was blind! He was … ' With a look of horror, Sunday pointed across the room.

Kate turned to look. A dark figure was stepping out arthritically from behind a statue. It was an old man, his eyes yellowed and clearly sightless. There was something old-fashioned about him: the loose cut of the dark suit that covered his portly frame; the small collar of his white shirt and tight knot in his tie; the fedora hat on his head. He looked like he'd just walked all the way from the 1940s. 'Is that him?' she hissed.

'No.' Sunday shook her head. 'But like him.'

'Who are you?' Kate demanded, unable to keep a waver from her voice.

'More to the point, young lady, who are you?' came an ancient, foreign-sounding voice behind her, dusty and scratchy with age.

Kate spun around to find another old man tottering out from the thick foliage that lined the wall behind her. He was taller and thinner, but dressed in the same style as his companion. His eyes were white and cloudy, flicking about uselessly in shrivelled sockets.

Sunday cried out and backed away, and Kate instinctively did the same. Stupid, she realised. The old man moved across to block their exit.

'What is this place?' Kate demanded.

'Why, it is our current abode,' said the portly man behind her. He too had a hard-edged accent, German perhaps, and his voice crackled like dead leaves. 'Takapa has taken good care to make us feel at home.' He gestured around him.

'We have to get out of here,' Sunday whispered. 'They're evil!'

'Come now, children,' said the withered figure blocking the exit, his unseeing eyes rolling in his head. He took a step towards them, fingers fumbling with the knot of his tie as he pulled it loose. 'We are just old men! Nothing more, eh, Anton?'

'Certainly, Friedrich,' agreed his companion jovially. 'That is all!'

Kate and Sunday backed away from the sinister

Friedrich, who tugged feebly at his collar buttons, as if only now aware of the heat.

Kate spun around to find Anton had already shed his jacket and tie, and now revealed a hairless, sunken chest as he stripped off his shirt. Kate stared in revulsion, knowing she and Sunday would soon be caught between these two old crazies.

'Well, Anton, it would seem that Takapa is truly pleased with our work,' wheezed Friedrich as he shrugged off his starched shirt.

'And with Liebermann's progress,' agreed Anton.

'How agreeable it is to be fed again so soon.' Friedrich moved aside a chair blocking his way. 'I find that appetite is one of the few things that does not diminish with age.'

'Stay back!' Kate shouted. She'd been such a fool. She'd thought that Takapa had no security here – wrong. He had these two freaks minding the store. And while they seemed elderly and frail, Kate wasn't going to leap to any more false conclusions. She pulled the flashlight from her pocket and held it like a miniature club. 'I'm warning you, stay back!'

But a low animal growl had begun to build. Kate turned to find that Anton had stooped over, and was stretching out his arms. His old bones twisted and snapped, rustling and cracking like ancient twigs. Coarse, wiry grey hair began to push its way out through the flaccid skin. His jaw elongated and snapped open and shut, pink gums dripping blood as decaying yellow teeth pushed through.

A snapping of jaws from the doorway made Kate turn again, to find Friedrich in the last throes of his metamorphosis. His lupine form was grey and rangy, ribs poking razor sharp through his lustreless fur, hind legs so skinny the 'wolf simply shuffled out of the smart black pants of the old-fashioned suit. Then it leaped for the cord that worked the lights, grabbed it in its jaws and yanked hard, shearing clean through the cable.

The room was plunged into darkness. Now they were all blind together.

Kate hurled the torch in the direction of the 'wolf at the exit, and heard it thud harmlessly into the foliage. She grabbed hold of Sunday's hand, tried to lead her away – but almost immediately she stumbled into a chair, and fell to the floor.

A scuffling of claws on carpet came from some-where nearby.

Kate scrambled up and allowed Sunday to drag her in a different direction – then Sunday cracked her head on something and stumbled to a halt.

'It's no good,' Kate whispered. 'They may be blind but they know where everything is in here – and *we're* just blundering around in the dark. We don't stand a chance!'

'They could finish us off any time,' Sunday whis-pered back. She gripped Kate's arm in the darkness. 'What are they waiting for?'

'They're playing with us,' Kate breathed. 'I don't imagine they have many visitors to snack on.'

As she spoke, her leg brushed against something, scaring her half to death – until she realised it was inanimate. Touching it, she discovered it was the ball pool. She'd had no idea they'd been herded so far across the penthouse.

A low, threatening growl started up, not far away.

Kate threw one of the small plastic balls into the darkness. It bounced off something hard with a clatter, one of the statues maybe. The growl stopped – the room fell entirely silent. Kate prayed the noise had confused the old 'wolves, made them think she and Sunday were actually the other side of the room.

But then the growl started up again; animal footsteps padded nearer.

Kate closed her eyes. It hadn't worked. She grabbed another ball and threw it in the direction of the growl.

It bounced off something just in front of her.

The growl became a roar and a slimy snout pushed into Kate's hand. Jagged teeth grazed her fingers as she recoiled in horror.

Sunday screamed at the top of her lungs.

The 'wolf skittered back a few paces, yelping and whining.

'They're sensitive to sound,' Kate realised. 'Sunday, keep screaming!'

Kate couldn't see Sunday but she could sure hear her oblige. As the ear-piercing shriek went on, Kate gathered up more balls from the pool in her arms.

'Hold out the hem of your sweater,' she hissed. Sunday did so with both hands, making a pouch into which Kate dumped the balls. 'Now, stay close behind me and let's holler like a pair of banshees!'

Using the position of the pool to get her bearings, Kate worked out where the exit must be. She tossed balls in front of her one at a time – if they hit nothing she moved forward. If they bounced back she threw another to the left or right to work out which way was clear.

Finally, she reached out and screamed for joy this

time, as her hand tightened on the door handle.

She swung the door open. As the light from outside spilled in, Kate had a nightmare glimpse of both 'wolves crouched close behind Sunday, scuttling forwards, their ears pressed down flat against their misshapen heads. Then Sunday was out of the room too and Kate slammed the door shut.

'Out of here,' Kate snapped, her voice reedy and hoarse from screaming. 'Now.'

Sunday bolted down the stairs without another word, the last few plastic balls falling from her sweater and clattering around after her.

Kate followed, never once looking back.

Tom kept apart from the other lupines in the corner of the careening truck. Luckily, all had kept their grotesque 'wolf forms, perhaps because the white wolves were uncaged, and so needed to be intimidated into submission. If they transformed back to their human shapes, Tom knew he would be expected to follow suit – and what then?

After an interminable, uncomfortable journey the truck came to a sudden halt. Metal gates squealed and rattled as they were opened, and the truck lurched forwards again. Soon after, Tom heard a thick, electrical whine and a resounding clang – he guessed a heavy door had come down behind them.

As the truck engine turned off, Tom recognised the chemical tang in the air, and also a damp, fusty smell – they must be at the back of United Laboratories.

The truck's doors were opened by two men, and Tom found they were parked in some kind of loading area. The men carried thick leather muzzles, and two metal crates waited behind them. The white wolves snapped and barked at the humans, but were silenced by an impressive roar from one of the lupines.

As the men fitted the wolves with muzzles, Tom jumped down from the van and skulked off into the thick shadows of the loading area. The other lupines followed him out, their work apparently done, and padded towards a doorway in one of the concrete walls. Tom decided to follow them.

It was some kind of changing room, a wide, echoing space lined with benches and lockers. Tom hovered outside, hearing bestial whimpers as the 'wolf-strength bled away from lupine bones, reverting back into human marrow. Having regained their human forms, the men were laughing about the guards they'd attacked, imagining the next day's papers putting the attacks down to escaped zoo animals, still on the loose ...

Once dressed, they sauntered out of the changing rooms, and Tom forced himself to change back. He shivered as he waited for the inevitable, sickening snap of his spine as it twisted back into shape, biting his lip as his pelvis cracked back into an upright position. His skin itched madly as the thick covering of hairs burrowed back under his skin.

Feeling weak and fatigued, he crept into the room and searched through lockers, helping himself to the first clothes he found that were his size – easy-fit blue jeans, a black track top and sneakers. Opening the door at the other end of the changing rooms, he realised his gamble had paid off. He'd made it inside Takapa's headquarters without attracting attention. At the back of his mind, the knowledge needled that the guy he'd impersonated could show up any time now and raise the alarm, but he forced himself to stay calm.

Ahead of him was a door that needed a security code – the entrance to United Laboratories, Tom guessed. To the side was a stairwell stretching up darkly to the next floor.

Tom made his way up the stairs to a long shabby corridor – and another door that needed a security code. He swore in frustration. He was about to make his way up the next flight of stairs when he heard footsteps approaching. There was a closet adjacent to the door. Tom stuffed himself in there, leaving the door open just a crack in the hope of catching the security code. The closet was airless and stank of bleach; it made him want to gag.

A man in a shabby white coat brushed past. Tom watched his fingers key in the code then push the door open and walk through. The door closed behind him with a muffled slam.

Tom waited a minute, then keyed in the same code. The door opened on to a stretch of corridor that ended in a further security door. He could hear a low moaning noise from somewhere up ahead, and sinister shuffling sounds. Holding his breath, he moved forwards.

The moaning was coming from behind a metal door halfway down. Tom gingerly tried the handle. The door was locked. But there was some sort of shutter at head height; an inspection hatch perhaps …

Tom slid the shutter across – and leaped back with a cry of shock.

A man's deathly-white face was pressed up against

the hatch. His eyes were wild and staring, his hair greasy and lank. 'Someone's here!' he shouted. He turned away to address another man Tom could now see slumped in a corner of the room. 'New guy.'

Tom saw both men were wearing grimy white coats and were similarly dishevelled.

The other man, wearing cracked glasses, rose from the filthy floor and elbowed aside the first. 'Have you brought us stuff?' Sores around his mouth cracked and bled as he spoke. 'Give it to us! You promised, you promised!' His voice was racked with desperation and despair. Both men began to beat on the door with raw knuckles.

Tom backed away, unnerved, unsure what to do. 'Who are you?' he asked hoarsely.

The man with glasses gave a sick grin. 'Don't you know? We're nobody now. Clever once. Scientists. Now we're nothing.'

Tom swallowed. 'Is ... is one of you called Dr John Walker?'

The first man reappeared, his face twisted in hatred. 'Dr Walker has yet to join us ... he's still Takapa's new favourite,' he sneered.

'But he'll wind up here one day. Just like the rest of us,' the other man added.

'I ... I can't stay,' Tom said, glancing around nervously. 'I might get caught.'

'Don't leave us!' the first man shouted pitifully. 'Give us what we need! You have to, you must!'

With a shudder Tom turned to head for the door leading back to the staircase. But just then, the door opened and a stooped old man in a dark suit and fedora hat entered.

Tom jumped back, bunching his fists as he realised it was the same man he'd seen holding the knife over Sunday. 'What is this?' he demanded. 'What the hell are you doing to these people?'

Unfazed, the man looked towards Tom, his bulbous nose twitching as he sniffed the air. He shuffled forward, yellowed teeth bared in a grotesque smile that never reached his clouded, ruined eyes. And then he began to speak – strange, guttural sounds that seemed scraped from the back of his throat.

Tom listened, strangely fascinated, as the screaming men began to quieten, their pleading giving way to sobs. Suddenly, he felt tired. So tired he could barely hold his eyes open. He became vaguely aware that the pitch of the old man's voice had changed, that his words had become longer, the sounds more complex.

Why am I even listening? A sharp dart of alarm tore through the fog in his mind but by then it was too late. He couldn't move. His legs wouldn't budge an inch.

CHAPTER NINE

'What have you done to me?' Tom asked, his words slurring. Had he been drugged, or hypnotised somehow?

'I have frozen the nerves to the muscles in your legs, arms and neck, inducing a temporary paralysis,' said the old man in a reedy, Germanic accent. 'You will not escape here again.'

Tom struggled and strained but he was helpless, completely unable to move. What the hell was happening to him? Tears of frustration welled up in his eyes.

The old man shuffled closer, and put his old, parched lips to Tom's ear. 'You spoiled a most promising experiment, boy, enabling the Walker girl to escape me. Perhaps I should close your windpipe little by little, suffocate you from the inside. I can do so with just a few words.' He chuckled. 'That might be an amusing diversion.'

In desperation Tom tried to bring on his change, tried to concentrate his anger, break the deadlock with the strength and power of his 'wolf.

The old man only tutted. 'Or perhaps I should string out the ecstasies of your lupine metamorphosis ... drag out the pain and the pleasure of the change over a few days, or a week – a month, perhaps.'

Tom felt wizened fingers caress the side of his head.

'How long before your mind snapped, I wonder. How long would it take ...'

'Longer than this one has to live, I'm afraid,' came a cold, familiar voice from the doorway.

Tom closed his eyes.

'It's good to see you, Tom,' said Marcie Folan. 'Takapa thought you'd have the sense to keep away while we had bigger fish to fry, but I knew you wouldn't disappoint me. So sweet of you to drop by ...'

He couldn't even shudder as she approached.

A prisoner in his own body.

Kate threw open the door to Blood's suite at the Drake, and she and Sunday collapsed gratefully inside.

Blood jumped up from a chair. 'Trolly! Sunday, are you all right? What did you find?'

'We found that Brook Mansion may be empty, but it has a couple of caretakers,' Kate told him with a shudder. 'What about you?'

'I've had better nights,' he sighed.

'Where's Tom?' asked Sunday.

Blood looked away. 'I don't know.'

'What?' Kate marched up to him. 'Is he all right? What happened?'

'This bloody great 'wolf came after us, we got separated and I tried to go after Tom – but by the time I caught up with him, all I saw was a van pulling away and another lupine who'd been left behind. So I bailed.' Blood sighed. 'Look, why don't I make us some of this excellent complimentary fresh roasted coffee and we can spill our collective beans.'

'Whatever,' Kate said. Sunday put a sympathetic hand on her shoulder, and Kate flashed her a cheerless smile.

They related their stories between bitter, scalding sips, Kate listening to Blood's patchy account with less and less patience.

'So, what exactly have we got to show for tonight?' Kate stormed. 'We were all nearly killed, none of us learned anything of any use and now poor Tom is—'

There was a sudden knocking at the door. 'Room service,' came a man's voice.

'Wrong room,' called Blood in his posh accent.

'It's your room number. I'll leave it outside,' the man said.

Blood swore under his breath and stomped over to see. But as he turned the handle the door flew open and struck him in the face. He staggered back as an Asian guy wearing black leathers and a silver wolf's head pinned on his chest charged in, flanked by three others wearing the same.

'Kate, Adam,' said Sunday, gesturing to the intruders, 'meet the Dark Chapter.'

'My name's Chung,' said the Asian guy. 'Fayn here's my deputy, my right-hand man.' He gestured briefly to the two other guys standing behind him. 'Zac and Mike, my enforcers.'

'Charmed, I'm sure,' said Blood, dabbing at his lip.

'Chung, huh?' Kate observed. 'Good pureblood name.'

He smiled.

'And I'm a *Fayn*,' the squinting guy reminded them, looking pissed off that he'd had to point out his pedigree.

'So what? I'm a Folan,' Kate said.

'Pureblood too, we know,' said Zac. Black and well-groomed, he was looking at Kate appreciatively. 'You're on the run with the wereling.'

'You helped kill your own brother,' added Chung. 'By rights, we should hand you over to your family, let justice be done.'

Sunday narrowed her eyes. 'Gee, you really are a good little bunch of boy scouts, aren't you?'

'Well, I think it's outrageous,' said Blood angrily, his posh persona lending him added confidence. 'Barging in like this while we're in the middle of enjoying a quite excellent cup of coffee. What were the Dark Chapter busy doing tonight? While Lincoln Park Zoo was going to the 'wolves, hmm?'

'That's why we're here,' said Chung. 'We know the wereling was involved in that crazy stunt down there tonight.'

'He took off with Takapa's crew,' added Fayn, 'together with the stolen white wolves. Why?'

'Because he's a brave little fool, I'd imagine,' said Blood hotly. 'We went there because we heard Takapa was up to something. You lot might not give a damn what he does so long as it doesn't impinge on your own agenda, but *we* do.' He paused. 'How do you know he went willingly?'

'I know someone who saw it,' said Fayn cockily. 'The guy was right there.'

'Interesting. I didn't think anyone saw that truck depart except me,' said Blood mildly. 'Oh, and the 'wolf from Takapa's crew who was left behind.'

Fayn frowned. 'What?'

'Didn't your contact tell you about that?' Blood

turned to Chung. 'I got separated from Tom. I went looking for him in the grounds, heard a vehicle pulling away, and went to investigate.' He glanced over at Fayn. 'It was night, and I was a long way off, but I most definitely saw a 'wolf run into the road. It chased after the truck but couldn't catch it – I thought it was Tom at first. Then it slunk off into the bushes.'

'I don't know anything about another 'wolf.' Fayn shrugged. 'Maybe my guy scrammed before he came along.'

'Well,' said Blood, 'speaking as one who *was* there to the end, I think Tom was accepted on board that truck because he bore a resemblance to the 'wolf left behind. In the heat of the moment, they didn't realise their mistake.'

'Seems we've wasted our time coming here,' said Chung. 'I thought the wereling could throw some light on the situation. Since he can't, we'll just have to pay Takapa a visit.'

Kate stared at him. 'And get Tom back? Rescue him?'

'Why should we?' asked Chung. 'He knew the score with Takapa.'

'Yeah,' chimed Zac. 'I mean, if he's dumb enough to hand himself over on a plate—'

'Or brave enough,' Kate broke in.

'In any case,' said Chung, 'it's time Takapa stopped trying to just suck up to my pureblood ass and accounted for himself. That stunt at the zoo, his people knocking out the security guards, leaving one of them for dead ...'

'He must be out of his mind,' agreed Zac. 'If these

guys start telling tales about men turning into 'wolves, and the press get a hold ...'

Blood clicked his tongue with fake sympathy. 'Could be a trifle inconvenient for the likes of you, couldn't it?'

'My ancestors spent their whole lives – *gave* them, sometimes – trying to keep the heat off of our kind,' said Chung solemnly. 'In this city, everyone answers to the Dark Chapter, Takapa included. It's time for a show of force.'

'So what, you storm his headquarters? All four of you?' Kate asked. 'Takapa will laugh in your face.'

'This is only the core of the Dark Chapter,' Chung told her impatiently.

'We've got a whole network in place around Chicago, keeping tabs on what's going on,' Fayn piped up. 'They've all got day jobs, all got family and loved ones to think about ... But when the call goes out, they'll drop everything – ready for action.'

'The Chapter comes first,' Chung added, and the others dutifully echoed the words.

'Jeez, you're like a bunch of little kids playing war, aren't you?' said Sunday.

'We do what we have to.' Chung shrugged. 'By dawn we'll have ourselves a small army.'

'I want to come with you,' Kate said.

'Why?'

'Because Tom might be in trouble. If you're going to be keeping Takapa's guards busy, there's a chance I'll be able to sneak in and find him.'

'You're crazy,' said Chung flatly. 'But I guess it's your life.'

'I want to come too,' said Sunday.

Mike gave her a patronising smile. 'We don't need a packed lunch, thanks.'

'My dad could be in there,' she insisted. 'I have to know.'

Chung stabbed a finger at Kate. 'She's a pureblood, she's got a right to be in on this. But you, girl, you're nothing but a liability.'

'So let her come,' suggested Blood, 'and if she's caught and killed, she's one less problem. Right?'

'Nice logic.' Chung's almond eyes narrowed to slits. 'Perhaps you should come too?'

Blood inclined his head. 'How could I resist such a charming invitation?'

'We'll be at the gates to his yard and ready to move at six,' said Chung. Then he turned and headed for the door, his men trailing after him in silence.

Once the door had slammed shut behind them, Kate pushed out a long, shaky breath and sat down on the couch. All she could think was, *What is happening to Tom right now?*

Sunday sat down beside her, her lower lip quivering, and Kate guessed she was wondering the same thing about her father.

'Was I rude not to offer them a cup of coffee?' Blood wondered aloud.

Tom watched cobwebbed ceilings go by high overhead as Marcie wheeled him through the corridors of Takapa's headquarters on a hospital trolley. The old man kept awkward pace a few metres behind.

'I used to do this a lot in my nursing days,' Marcie announced. 'Take my drowsy patients off to the operating room, ready for their surgery.'

'Surgery?' Tom asked hoarsely. He felt sick with fear. His arms and legs were still locked in place, dead and useless; he'd never felt so helpless. The creepy old man hadn't taken away his power of speech, but Tom found it hard to get his tongue around the words. 'So what have you been doing, tucked away here for so long?' Tom asked Marcie, his voice slurring like he'd just had a bad trip to the dentist. 'Licking your wounds after Jicaque thrashed you in New York?'

'It was a setback, I'll admit. But breeding a drug-dependent army was just one element of Takapa's grand design,' said Marcie. 'It's a flexible program. Its aims and priorities change according to circumstances.'

'Sure they do,' Tom said. 'And *without* your little army of junkie gladiators, hiding out in this lovely part of town has been priority number one.' He swallowed down thick saliva and glared up at her. 'So why are you torturing those scientists? Just to pass the time?'

'Torture?' Marcie shook her head. 'We give them bliss.'

'Bliss in a needle,' muttered Tom. 'I know those symptoms. You've got them hooked on that same serum you used in New York. But ... I thought Jicaque had spoiled your supply?'

'We had sufficient stock in Chicago for our needs,' said Marcie. Then she gave a theatrical sigh. 'Those scientists were so drearily stubborn about not doing what we wanted when they first arrived here. They needed some ... *persuasion*. The drug makes them remarkably compliant.'

'It makes them into blood-crazed wrecks,' Tom retorted.

'It's important they stay motivated,' said Marcie

blandly. 'Deadlines are tight, and we've been hot-housing a number of important projects here.'

'Like Project Resurrection?' he guessed, remembering what Sunday had told him.

'Always so inquisitive.' Marcie bared her teeth in an unpleasant smile. 'The temporary termination of our plans in New York came at a fortuitous time. We have been able to channel our energies – and those of our workforce – into something that will further our cause to a far greater extent.'

Tom didn't like the sound of that.

Marcie wheeled the trolley through a set of double doors, and into a large, white room completely at odds with the other areas of the dingy warehouse he'd seen. It was somewhere between Frankenstein's laboratory and an ultramodern operating room. Modern microscopes and slim laptop computers shared work-benches with smoking, bubbling beakers heated by bunsens and clunky equipment that looked old enough to be steam-powered.

Then, from behind an inelegant bank of baffling equipment, a man emerged.

'Hal Folan,' Tom croaked, recognising Marcie's husband – and Kate's father. 'Just like old times, isn't it?'

Hal glared at him uncomfortably. With a cursory nod to the old man, who was wheezing softly out of Tom's sight, he asked his wife, 'Where's Kate?'

'She's not with him,' said Marcie. 'He got in un-detected by duping those imbeciles who stole the white wolves.'

'Resourceful,' Hal observed with clinical detachment. 'But then, we've always known that.' He walked in front of Tom's line of vision to stand before two large observation windows looking into an adjoining room.

From his position on the trolley, Tom was just about high enough to see through. In there two people, anonymous and sexless in white gowns and headgear, were hunched over a twitching animal, reaching periodically for one of the gleaming surgical instruments in the tray beside them.

'How is Walker doing?' enquired Marcie.

'He's prepared the enhanced genetic material from the white wolf,' said Hal. 'Just finishing up.'

'Walker?' Tom breathed. 'That's John Walker, Sunday's father?'

'Our brightest recruit. His studies of stem cells and their healing qualities have proven invaluable to our work here.'

'Really,' Tom said. His throat felt thick and constricted – he had to really concentrate to push out the words. 'I'll bet he's just thrilled he could help.'

Marcie chuckled softly. 'Such an elegant idea of Takapa's, don't you think? He opens United Laboratories, offering generous grants to attract bright, cutting-edge doctors and scientists ... steers their research, then utilises their discoveries ...'

'And once they get an idea of what he's really up to, he imprisons them here and dopes them up.' Tom gave her a disgusted look, which he hoped was more eloquent than his slurred speech. 'Existing only for their next fix of serum.'

Marcie snapped her jaws together. 'You really shouldn't fret about those poor, tortured souls back there. They'll know some peace, soon enough.' She smiled coldly. 'You'd do better to worry about yourself.'

'What's Walker doing in there?' asked Tom slowly. 'Why did you steal the white wolves?'

'Their genes hold information that may be valuable,' Marcie told him.

Just then, the door opened behind them, and Tom heard something heavy being wheeled inside. He frowned as a severe-looking woman, so thin she resembled a stick insect in a skirt, stalked into view.

'Marcie, where do you want *this* to go?' the woman asked in a petulant voice, gesturing distastefully behind her.

'Ah, Araminta. Is this the new subject for Liebermann's experiment?'

Araminta nodded. 'Drugged and sleeping like a fat baby.'

Marcie tutted at Tom. 'You rescued the Walker girl, so we simply *had* to find another subject.'

Tom watched as a large man in a wheelchair was wheeled into the room by a sour-faced lackey. The man in the chair wore a security guard's uniform, and his many chins quivered as he snored softly.

'This was not one of the temp agency's great successes,' Araminta reported. 'I don't tolerate incompetents on my gallery staff. Nevertheless, he is fitting for our purpose. He has no family, and few friends who'll mourn him ... and in any case, he'd only create a bad impression on patrol at the gallery when our pureblood patrons come to visit.'

'Well, Liebermann?' asked Marcie. 'Will he do?'

Liebermann, the old blind man, tottered forwards and felt the unconscious guard's face and body, like a butcher might probe a side of meat. Then he gave a throaty chuckle. 'He certainly offers a good deal of material to work with.' He turned to the lackey. 'Leave him in the corner.' The miserable-looking man obeyed, then left silently.

'All we need now is a corpse,' said Liebermann softly.

'Come dawn, you shall have as many as you need,' Marcie promised him.

Hal tore his gaze away from the observation window for a moment, noticed Araminta apparently for the first time, and nodded his head in formal, almost wary, greeting.

Araminta walked over to Tom, her spindly heels tapping harshly on the tiled floor, and regarded him coldly. 'This must be the boy you mentioned. He doesn't look like anything special.'

'It's what's inside that counts,' cooed Marcie, tracing a talon lightly down Tom's cheek. 'The secrets of his DNA have intrigued us for some time.'

'Walker's finished,' Hal announced suddenly, wringing his hands like an expectant father in the labour ward. 'They're coming out!'

The two figures in their surgical smocks entered the room from the operating theatre through a metal doorway. Tom could tell instantly that one of them was John Walker; Sunday had his startling blue eyes and the same high forehead. But when he pulled down his facemask, he looked far older than Tom had pictured, his face strained and almost grey with fatigue. And there was a mark on his neck. A puncture wound. He'd been bitten.

Tom felt a fresh surge of hatred for his captors. Any man or woman was an acceptable target for these monsters. They took whoever they wished, wrenched them away from the lives they had known and the people who loved them – and placed their hateful, bloody curse upon them. Tom thought of Stacy Stein's husband, who'd killed himself when his bloodlust grew uncontrollable; of his parents having to face up to Christmas without him; of all the powerless 'wolf-victims he'd met in New York – and felt his anger deepen and grow...

Still his frozen body refused to budge an inch.

'You were successful, I trust?' enquired Marcie.

'I think so,' said Walker wearily. 'Combining the wolf and human genes is a highly demanding procedure. But the König Man's DNA samples don't seem to be rejecting the genetic material from the white wolves.'

Hal placed his hand on the scientist's arm. 'His body can be fully restored?'

'I believe so. With this pure wolf DNA it should be possible, using very aggressive gene therapies, to reverse the damage to the body tissue.'

'You're certain?' hissed Marcie. 'You said the work would be complete long before now.'

'How could I have foreseen the problems we'd have regenerating the body?' snapped Walker. 'I've never experimented on lupine tissue before.' He grew more subdued under Marcie's withering glare.

'Do as we ask and you will get the serum you crave,' said Marcie. 'Refuse and you will get nothing.'

Emotions flitted pathetically across Walker's face: hatred, desire, self-disgust.

They've got him totally hooked, Tom realised. *He'll do everything they ask and more.*

'Please, John,' Hal said quietly. 'We must know. Time is running out. If we – if Takapa is to fulfil his aims ...'

Walker nodded miserably. He pressed a phial into Hal's hand then trudged back towards the operating room with his assistant.

As they went through the open door Tom saw it was a white wolf on the operating table, its fur glowing almost silver under the harsh multiple lights.

Hal held the phial up to the light. 'Yes,' he breathed. 'Yes, the skin is rejuvenating already. Look!' He passed the phial to Marcie. 'Pink and fresh. Takapa will be most pleased.'

'And not a moment too soon,' Araminta murmured. 'The purebloods will be arriving at Brook Mansion at noon tomorrow, ready for the preliminary briefing ...'

'There have been so many delays,' worried Hal. 'Walker's exhausted – he may make mistakes. I still say Takapa should have delayed this gathering until we were certain of—'

'Takapa knows what he is doing, my dear,' insisted Marcie coldly. 'He is *fully* confident of success.'

Tom cleared his claggy throat. 'Remind me, Hal ... is she hitched to you, or Takapa? Only she seems pretty into that albino freak—'

Hal's face darkened. 'Be silent!' he shouted.

Even Marcie seemed startled. She opened her mouth as if to speak, then faltered and closed it again.

Raw nerve, Tom noted.

Liebermann gave a thin chuckle, and moved closer to the unconscious security guard. 'I am sure, Folan, you will feel happier come the dawn, when my colleagues join me to perform the ritual on this flabby creature.' Then he glared at Tom. 'The boy spoiled my experiment at an early stage this morning. But I remain confident of the ultimate outcome.'

'Speaking of "this one" ...' said Marcie meaningfully.

Liebermann nodded. 'There are perhaps other duties we must attend to,' he said quietly.

Marcie looked down gloatingly at Tom. 'You'll remember why we turned you 'wolf in the first place, I'm sure ... A mate for our only daughter; an injection of new blood to stabilise our pureblood genepool.'

Tom twisted his head awkwardly away from her.

'Nothing's changed, my little wereling,' she said more softly. 'Only now I have lent my support to Takapa, I can draw on his resources, and simply remove what I need from you in a single, straightforward procedure.' She leaned in close, and Tom could smell rank, raw meat on her breath. 'Your nature is rare, Tom. You draw on the best of your humanity and the best of the 'wolf. A thinking, calculating beast not dependent on instinct alone.'

'Flattery will get you nowhere,' Tom said thickly. It was getting harder and harder to talk.

She went on. 'Once we have cracked your genetic code we shall use it to genetically enhance the offspring Kate shall bear Takapa ... Their children will grow to be true champions of the lupine race.' She sniggered. 'Kate will be such a proud mother, don't you think?'

Tom's throat was burning and words wouldn't form in his mouth any longer. Summoning all his strength, he spat in her face.

Marcie wiped her eye with a bony hand, her smile

still frozen in place. 'Walker,' she called. 'Get in here.'

He shuffled out sulkily from the theatre. 'More interruptions?'

'A chance for you to earn your next fix ahead of schedule,' she said calmly. 'Your assistant can continue your other tasks in your absence. Prepare to operate on the boy. Hal will tell you what we need from him.'

Araminta and Hal both looked uncomfortable as Walker crossed obediently to a sink and began to wash his hands.

But Liebermann was smiling. He shuffled over to Tom. 'I shall administer the anaesthetic at once,' he said.

'And when you wake, Tom, you'll be mine to kill at last,' said Marcie softly. 'It will be slow ... and it will hurt you so very much. And with every cut, with every chunk we tear from your body, Hal and I will remember the son you took from us ...'

Tom felt a single tear escape and roll down his left cheek, as the old man started reciting his dark script. Then all he knew was the chill of his fear, before blackness.

CHAPTER TEN

Kate huddled down further into her coat, feeling the cold dawn seep into every bone. It was Christmas Eve. Peace and goodwill to all men.

She watched Chung's friends tool up with baseball bats and knuckledusters from the back of his white van. It was creepy, somehow; these respectable-looking men and women all looked like they belonged down at the playground with their kids, or in a swish office somewhere, clinching deals – not getting ready to start what was promising to be a very messy fight.

Soon, a sea of black leather began to encroach on Takapa's yard. Mike sliced through the chain on the yard gates with some lethal-looking cutters.

Blood watched the scene dispassionately, his floppy dark hair bouncing around in the cold wind like it was caught up in some private crisis. 'Sunday, when the 'wolves captured you here ... did they take you in through the yard?'

'No. There's an alley around the side that leads to a fire door,' answered Sunday through chattering teeth. 'More private, I guess. I got out that way too, when Tom ...' She trailed off. 'Why d'you ask?'

Kate cast her a sideways glance. 'Even if Chung does manage to get us all inside, that yard will be the first place the 'wolves secure once we're in – to keep us from getting back out the same way.'

'By George, I think she's got it,' said Blood approvingly.

'We're ready,' announced Chung to the gathered crowd, quite calm and confident. 'Remember, this is a show of strength. We're not here to start a war, but to *prevent* one. These people are our brothers.' Fayn offered him a pick handle, and Chung accepted it, weighing it in both hands. 'Only use force if you have to.'

The crowd nodded and muttered, but Kate noticed that they never relaxed their grip on their weapons for a moment. Chung led them into the yard, his followers fanning out into a semi-circle behind him as they approached the main doors. Kate felt her stomach twist with nerves as she, Sunday and Blood lingered at the back of the ugly mob.

Chung was conferring with Fayn and Zac, pointing at the main doors – when they abruptly burst open. Three men darted out. Two grabbed Chung and lifted him clear off the ground before he could even react. The other man grabbed Fayn and snatched him inside. Chung kicked and yelled to be released as he was hauled bodily into the building.

At the same moment, three 'wolves bolted out of the dark maw of the building, jaws slavering, yellow eyes gleaming. Without hesitation they tore into the startled crowd. Bodies went down, claws swiped and teeth scissored through flesh. Blood started to spurt and splatter. Then two more 'wolves, dark, hulking scabrous creatures, lurched out, drool stringing down from their jaws.

Sunday grabbed hold of Kate's arm, backed away into Blood. 'It's an ambush! Like they knew Chung was coming!'

'Someone's sold him out,' Kate said. She saw Mike's prone body trampled by one of the 'wolves, heard Zac yelling as he brought an iron bar down on the back of a black, shambling lupine creature, only to be dragged down by the raking claws of another of the beasts.

'Come on,' said Blood, ushering them both towards the gates. 'That side door Sunday mentioned, quick.'

Kate stared at him. 'What?'

'The 'wolves were obviously told to expect an assault on the yard, and they're dealing with it. If they're acting on information, they won't be expecting anyone to enter through the fire door.'

'You hope,' said Sunday.

She led Kate and Blood around to the chain-link fence at the end of the alleyway that led to the fire door. Kate started to scale it, climbing clumsily but swiftly, the links biting into her numb fingers. Blood was close behind her, but Sunday was struggling.

'I hate heights,' she moaned. 'I pushed underneath last time but they've closed up the gap.'

'Just climb like there's a werewolf right behind you,' Blood snapped, 'because as soon as they've dealt with Chung's friends in the yard, there could be.'

Without another word, Sunday started climbing. Kate followed Blood down to the end of the alley. The fire door was sealed shut.

Blood hammered on the door with his fist. 'It worked, lads,' he shouted. 'They fell for it! It's all over out there, come and see!'

The door opened and a man's eager face came into

view. Blood planted his fist in the middle of it.

As the guard fell back inside and collapsed to the concrete, Kate flung open the door to reveal another man lunging towards them. She kicked the man's ankle from under him and he fell to the ground. Before he could rise, Sunday came sprinting down the alleyway and jumped on his head with both feet. The man stayed down.

'The advantages of not dieting,' quipped Sunday shakily.

'Come on,' said Blood, pushing his hair from his eyes. 'You're the one with local knowledge, Sunday. Where might Tom and your dad be?'

'I was being held on the first floor,' she said. 'Until they took me to that room up at the top for the ceremony stuff.'

Kate shuddered, and pulled the fire door back closed. 'We'd better get looking,' she said, heading up the cold and echoing stairway. 'From the way the fight was going out front, we won't have a distraction for long.'

The place seemed deserted, the corridors silent save for the hum of the fluorescents above. Kate's stomach was a tight knot as she and Sunday trailed behind Blood, checking doors as they went. But there were so many rooms to look into, mostly nondescript store-rooms or shabby offices, and the minutes were ticking by ...

Kate saw a bright blush of light on the floor beneath a set of white double doors. She pushed them open and saw Tom's body on a hospital trolley, his head protruding from a white shroud. For a second her heart seemed to spin in her chest, elated that she'd found him. Then her hand flew to her mouth. 'Oh, Tom ...' she breathed.

'Shit,' said Sunday.

Kate felt Blood's hands comfortingly on her shoulders, but she brushed them off and flew over to where Tom lay, white-faced, eyes tightly shut. She took his wrist, felt for a pulse; it was like handling ice.

She pressed her cheek against his dry lips, and caught the faint brush of his breath. 'He's alive,' she croaked, looking up at Sunday and Blood with hope in her eyes. She rocked him gently. 'Tom? Wake up, Tom, it's Kate.'

He didn't stir.

'Tom!' she hissed in his ear. '*Please*, wake up ... for God's sake!'

Blood was indicating gravely across the room. Kate looked up and saw two windows that looked on to an operating room.

'They've gone to work on him,' said Blood.

'Can we move him?' whispered Sunday.

'We're going to have to,' said Blood, coming across to join Kate by Tom's body. He gripped her by the shoulders. 'We *must* get him outside.'

Sunday made a dry squeaking noise at the back of her throat. 'My dad ...'

Blood turned to her awkwardly. 'Look, I'm sorry, Sunday. I know you're worried sick about your dad but if we don't get Tom—'

'He's here,' she said, dully. 'Dad's here.' She was walking through into the operating room.

Kate quickly followed her.

A man who looked to be about sixty was slumped back in a chair, looking up at the ceiling, hands clenching and unclenching by his sides. The spit trail from his sagging mouth sparkled in the harsh surgical lights. Kate recalled the comforting smell of cherry tobacco in Walker's car, tried to reconcile the homely image it had conjured in her mind with this harsh, haggard apparition before her now.

'Dad?' Sunday took his uncomprehending fist in her hand. 'Dad, it's me!'

His eyes came down from the ceiling to regard her glassily. 'Who are you?' he asked.

Sunday recoiled as if he'd struck her. 'It ... it's *me*, Dad.'

'Don't play games with me!' His hand twisted out of hers and grabbed hold of her wrist. 'Marcie sent you. Have you got it? The serum?'

'Dad, you're hurting me!' Sunday tried to pull free, but Kate saw his fingers were digging down vice-like into her flesh. 'Dad, please!'

'Useless girl!' he spat at her. 'I'm doing nothing more for you people until I get my fix. Understand?' His eyes were wild, his breath harsh and ragged. Finally he let go of Sunday's arm, shoved her away from him. 'Nothing! I'm not digging out samples from anyone else until—'

'Digging out samples?' Kate's breath caught in the back of her throat. 'Then it was *you*. What did you do to Tom?'

'What did I do?' Walker started sobbing pathetically. 'I did everything Marcie told me to. She promised me ... promised me it would be all right ...'

Kate balled her fists. 'I said, what did you do?'

'It wasn't him!' protested Sunday. 'Tell her, Dad.'

He shrugged. 'Stuck in the needle, pulled things out.'

He scowled. 'And still the bitch gives me nothing.'

'Dad, you don't know what you're saying!' Sunday rubbed at her bruised arm. 'We've got to get out of here, come *on* ...'

While Sunday spoke to her father in a low, coaxing voice, Kate noticed some phials in a steel tray in the corner of the room. There were little grey and pink shavings floating in fluid inside them; a clue to whatever the hell Walker was working on, perhaps. If Stacy ever showed up, she might be able to make something of them.

As she slipped one into the pocket of her black trousers, a menacing growl started up. She swung around, looking for the source of the sound, and saw a cage under the table behind her. A snow-white wolf was crushed inside, staring out at her with narrowed eyes. At its feet, an identical wolf lay prone on its side.

Kate turned on Walker. 'These poor animals ...'

'I only do what I'm told,' he said wretchedly. 'Funny, isn't it? We're just the same, under the skin ... both locked up, both helpless ...'

'Dad?' Sunday reached out for his hand. 'What ... what are you saying?'

'I'm not going anywhere until I get some of that drug,' shouted Walker. 'So just leave me alone.' He shifted in the chair, trying to turn his back on them.

Kate saw the dark scab that clung to Walker's neck.

'That wound,' said Sunday, slowly, her eyes glistening. 'They ... have they ...?'

Kate nodded. 'I'm so sorry, Sunday,' she said, hugging the girl as she dissolved into tears. 'This is what Takapa's 'wolves do. How they make people act for them.'

'No,' moaned Sunday. 'No, no, no, no ...'

'You'd better get in here, you two,' called Blood.

With a last pitying look at Walker, curled up in the chair and lost in his own nightmare world, Kate steered Sunday back out to Blood.

He was looking at a dark, sunken lump in a wheelchair.

Kate recognised the uniform through the gore smeared over it. Saw the wisps of ginger hair sticking up from the mulch stuck to the back of the chair.

She turned and retched, clutching her stomach. 'The security guard from the gallery.'

'It would seem Tom got off lightly,' said Blood quietly.

'I can't stand any more of this,' said Sunday, wiping tears and snot from her face. 'This isn't happening. None of this can be happening.'

'I'm so pleased to hear that,' said Blood dryly. 'Maybe we'll all wake up safe and sound at the Drake, any moment now. But just in case ...' He grabbed a medical case filled with scalpels and other nasty-looking medical instruments and placed them on Tom's chest. 'In case we run into trouble on our way out of here.' Seeing Kate's shocked expression he flashed a bleak smile at her. 'Help me with the trolley, Trolly.'

Kate nodded, took hold of the feet end and helped Blood steer Tom out through the double doors.

Sunday hesitated in the doorway, her eyes red and puffy. 'I can't just leave Dad here!'

'Look,' Kate said, trying to stay calm. 'We'll get Tom out first, then come back for your dad, see if we can convince him to—'

But even as she spoke, Walker jumped up from the chair and turned to face them. 'It's a test, isn't it?' he said, staggering closer. 'I have to earn the stuff – that's what Marcie keeps saying.' He stared at them blankly, his voice rising with desperation. 'Well, all right, then. I'll earn it.'

'Oh, Dad, no!' shrieked Sunday.

Kate saw Walker's form begin to shift, saw his haggard face sprout thick hair and twist into something alien, bestial. He gave a choking, guttural roar and hunched forwards, his lab coat splitting into tatters, his hands splaying out and sprouting fearsome claws. In the cage behind him, the remaining white wolf began to whine and bark. Disturbed, it clawed against the wire.

'Great Gorgon buttocks,' breathed Blood. Darting back, he grabbed the wheelchair that held the security guard's remains and charged at Walker. The heavy chair crashed into the scientist, sending him sprawling. He cracked his head against the workbench. The pile of human remains upended over him, burying his changing shape.

'Out of here!' ordered Blood, shoving the trolley with all his force. 'Now!'

'You killed him!' yelled Sunday.

'I doubt that,' said Blood. 'But he'll do a better job on us if we don't move it. And keep your sodding voice down!'

They turned the corner, heading for the exit at the end of the corridor. Still the place seemed silent and empty.

But it wasn't.

As they neared the stairwell door, a slim, haughty

figure detached itself from the shadows and stood in front of them, barring their way.

'Stand very still, please,' said Araminta Black, pointing a gun at Blood's head. 'You were right – you really should have stayed quiet. You've made enough noise to wake the dead.' She smiled slyly. 'And that's our job.'

Kate was all for taking a chance and running the skinny bitch down, but Blood had frozen as requested, looking at the gun barrel apprehensively. Kate saw that Araminta was quite collected and calm, fixing him with an unnerving stare. She knew with sick certainty that this woman would not hesitate to kill them.

Behind them the caged wolf's whining grew louder, more frantic.

'I suppose it's too late to apologise about my behaviour in your gallery yesterday?' enquired Blood. 'It really has been on my conscience.'

'Your conscience won't be bothering you much longer,' said Araminta. She jerked the gun and advanced on them. 'I'm glad I came now. I wanted to watch the festivities out there ... I didn't think I'd get to take part in some fun of my own.'

Blood and Sunday led the slow retreat back up the corridor. Kate brushed her fingers against Tom's pale, clammy face as she was forced away from the trolley. After all they'd been through, it had to be the lousiest goodbye in history.

Araminta was herding them back towards the theatre, and now she stood between Kate and the trolley, blocking her last view of Tom's prone body.

Always the 'wolves, coming between them.

A howl of anguish carried from the theatre. Not the white wolf this time.

Walker.

Sunday started to sob. Kate heard the sharp scrape of claws scrabbling against a tiled floor.

For a moment Araminta frowned in confusion. Then she smiled. 'Why, you must've made Dr Walker cross,' she said, her frog-like eyes shining with an unearthly gold light. She indicated to the doorway with the gun. 'Perhaps you should go back inside. Kiss and make up?'

Blood slipped his arms protectively around Kate and Sunday, as the 'wolf behind the doors scuttled closer.

CHAPTER ELEVEN

Kate saw Araminta's grip on the gun tighten as she opened her mouth to speak again. But the words never came. There was a loud thud and the spindly woman jerked forwards, collapsing on the floor at Kate's feet. Kate looked up in disbelief.

Tom was still lying prone on the trolley. But he'd picked up the box of medical instruments that Blood had put on his chest and swung his arms backwards over his head. The sharp corner of the box had smashed against Araminta's skull.

'Tom!' Kate cried, and ran to his side. He looked like death warmed up, but he was smiling at her.

'Paralysis wearing off,' he croaked. 'I can move my arms.'

'Your aim is good too,' beamed Blood. 'Miss Black is out cold.'

But Tom didn't answer. The box fell from his grip with a noisy crash as he lapsed again into sleep, his face as white as the shroud that covered him.

Sunday shrieked suddenly as a dark, rangy shape burst out through the double doors and turned to face them. Its jaws and muzzle were wet and black with detritus from the guard's corpse.

'Which reminds me,' added Blood. 'We were in the

middle of a daring escape before we were so rudely interrupted. Shall we?'

Kate was already grabbing the tail end of Tom's trolley and pulling it away back towards the stairwell. Blood lent his weight and they set off down the corridor. Sunday raced ahead of them, still sobbing, and threw open the door.

Kate turned around to see if Walker was following them. But he was hunched over Araminta's limp body, trying to tear off her jacket.

'He doesn't give a shit about us,' said Sunday savagely. 'He's just hoping she's got some of that damned drug.'

Kate could find no comfort to offer her. 'Help me with Tom,' she muttered, as she and Blood fought to find an angle that would allow the trolley through the doorway. There would be time for tears and sympathy later.

If they actually got out of this place alive.

Tom was aware of his deliverance from Takapa's lair only in snatches.

His back jarred and hurt as the trolley juddered down the stone steps. He felt sick. Heard an echoing crash, then he was looking up at a grey wintry sky. The cold felt good on his hot face. Wetness. A fine rain was falling; yesterday's snow would melt.

The trolley sped along uneven ground, the wheels catching on stones. A tall fence loomed out of white mist. He was being lifted from the trolley. Blood's cologne in his nostrils, too strong. Blood was carrying him over his shoulder. He heard raised voices but the sounds were distorting. Hands were pulling at him, pushing at him, he was jerked up through the air. His body felt like it was on fire, and the spinning world went black.

When he woke again he was in the back of a car, propped up and shivering on the back seat. Kate was beside him.

'Tom? Tom, are you OK?' Kate sounded worried.

Tom kind of liked to hear that concern in her voice over him. He felt maybe he should tell her, but the words wouldn't come.

Words. The old man's voice filling his head. Blocking off sights and sounds, the pain of Walker's knife—

He clutched at Kate, yelled out. Felt the car lurch as someone stamped on the brakes.

And suddenly the world was clear again. He saw Mike from the Dark Chapter slumped beside Kate in the back seat. He looked sick and stern, there were three deep red scores in his pale neck and his white T-shirt was soaked with blood. Sunday was in the passenger seat, her hair hanging down over her blotchy face, her eyes swollen and puffy from crying.

Tom realised Blood was looking at him, searchingly. 'I'm sorry,' he said, sinking back into the car seat. The stiff white smock he wore chafed against his skin.

'Don't be,' Kate said, running her hand through his damp hair. 'I think you just came out of your fever.'

'Good job too,' said Blood with mock severity, 'because we're almost back at the hotel, and I'm damned if I'm going to carry you another step. Getting you over that fence was bloody murder ...'

Blood pulled back out into the traffic. Tom's gaze settled again on Mike. 'So what's he doing here?'

'Getting the hell away from Takapa's place,' Kate said, 'just like the rest of us.'

'It was a massacre,' said Mike hoarsely. 'They killed Zac ... killed so many of us ...'

'What were you expecting?' enquired Blood. 'Fisticuffs by Queensberry Rules?'

'There was no need for it,' Mike shouted, smashing his fist against the door. 'No need to lay into us like that.'

'I guess the people you've hunted and killed thought something similar,' said Sunday, quietly and coldly.

Kate briefly explained to Tom what had happened in the yard.

'Someone must've told Takapa exactly what Chung was planning,' Tom realised.

'Gee, do you really think so?' Kate deadpanned, giving his hand a squeeze.

'Bullshit,' muttered Mike, clenching his fists. 'None of us would ever do that.'

'I wonder where Chung and Fayn are now,' muttered Tom.

Mike shrugged. 'Still inside, I guess ... I was knocked out for a while. When I woke up, the 'wolves were too busy chewing bones to notice me sneak off.'

'Guess they exceeded their kill quota, huh?' Tom said without much sympathy. 'Wolves weren't his favourite people right now.

'They must need Chung for something,' Kate mused, 'or else they would've killed him out in the yard.'

'I've got to get out of here,' said Mike. 'This is my business, not yours. I'll work it out my way.'

'I think you made it my business,' snapped Sunday, 'when you decided it would be OK for Tom to eat me like a goddamned steak.'

'I said stop the car,' shouted Mike, ignoring her. 'I

need some air ... space to think by myself.'

Blood slowed down, and Mike launched himself from the back of the Merc, striding out into the horn-blaring traffic like he just didn't see it.

Kate reached across and pulled the door shut.

Blood sighed. 'You know, I actually feel sorry for the poor sod.'

A smothering silence descended on the car. Tom looked out the window at the shops' festive window displays, at the twinkling fairy lights stretched across the street, at the last-minute Christmas shoppers bustling busily by. It felt like they were a million miles away, in another world.

'What did they do to you, Tom?' whispered Kate.

'I don't know.' His eyes were growing heavy again. As his thoughts spiralled back down into sleep, he was barely aware of Kate's fingers as they intertwined with his own.

Wanted criminal or not, Kate was too tired to care a damn about the funny looks she got – staggering through the hotel reception with a boy in a surgical smock, a girl in tears and a man with a gleaming smile waving at surprised onlookers like he was some film star gracing them with his presence.

In the elevator, the smile dropped from Blood's face. 'We need to get out of here,' he said. 'Your mother and Takapa must know we're here by now.'

Sunday nodded. 'Chung will have told them if nothing else.'

'We're too vulnerable,' Kate agreed, her arm tightly around the barely-conscious Tom. 'Especially with Tom like this.'

'We'll leave a note in reception for your friends,' said Blood, as the elevator reached their floor. 'With strict instructions they only hand it over to an old Native American medicine man ...'

The doors slid smoothly open and Blood helped Kate support Tom for the short walk to their door.

But the door stood ajar.

'We're too late,' whispered Sunday.

'Back the way we came,' mouthed Blood, and Kate nodded. She turned, and gasped.

An old man was standing behind them.

A short, scruffy Native American whose silver hair hung down to his shoulders in straggling braids. His face was lined, his nose like an eagle's beak, his cleft chin strong and jutting. His amber eyes sparkled as he held out his arms to Kate and smiled.

'Jicaque,' Kate breathed, ready to collapse with relief.

'I hope you will forgive us not waiting in reception,' he said in his warm, halting voice. 'But we thought we'd better keep a lower profile, away from prying eyes.' He frowned as he took in the scene. 'What has happened to Tom?'

'We're hoping you can tell us,' said Blood, lapsing instantly into posh mode as he always did with new-comers. 'How'd you get behind us like that? The coast was clear a moment ago.'

'Forgive me, Mr Blood,' said Jicaque, relieving Kate of Tom's deadweight and helping him inside the hotel suite. 'I am guilty at times of showing off.'

'Jeez, what happened to him?' came a familiar voice with a Bronx twang to it.

They turned back to face the open door. Stacy Stein was standing there.

'Let me guess,' said Blood, raising an eyebrow at this latest newcomer. 'Stacy Stein?'

'You got it.' Stacy flashed him a crooked smile as she helped Jicaque lay Tom down on the bed and checked his pulse. She was in her early thirties, her cute-but-careworn features framed by coppery shoulder-length hair, and dressed in black trousers and a grey sweater. 'Hey, Kate. What the hell has Tom been doing?'

Kate gave her a brief explanation and a hug, then made hurried introductions to Blood and Sunday.

Jicaque didn't respond to the pleasantries, applying delicate pressure with his fingers to Tom's skull. It was obvious he was worried.

'His pulse is weak,' noted Stacy.

'And his heart is erratic,' Jicaque observed. Gently he rolled Tom on to his side. 'And there is an ... energy surrounding him.'

'You worry about his aura,' said Stacy dourly, raising the smock and studying some livid cuts on Tom's bare back. 'I'm more worried about these wounds. And look at this mark on his spine. Lumbar puncture, I'm guessing.'

Sunday frowned. 'Then they extracted cerebrospinal fluid?' When Stacy gave her an approving glance, she shrugged. 'My dad used to be a doctor.'

'He's 'wolf now,' Kate told Jicaque. 'You have to help him.'

'There is much I have to do,' said Jicaque coolly. 'But first I must minister to the boy.'

Stacy rolled her eyes. 'And do what? Give him a herb to chew on?'

Her sarcasm seemed lost on Jicaque, who was now dangling some kind of charm over Tom's chest.

'My medicine is best for him now. Great power has been exerted on his nervous system to stop him struggling.'

'Magic?' asked Sunday timidly.

'Give me a break, there are needle marks on his arm,' said Stacy. 'Anaesthetic, maybe? Blood samples?'

'Back in New Orleans,' said Blood, 'Takapa tried to have Tom operated on, to find out more about what makes him a wereling.'

'I remember,' Kate said with a shiver.

'Well, this time … I reckon he's done it.'

'It's possible Tom's had a bad reaction to an anaesthetic,' agreed Stacy. 'The symptoms are—'

'No ordinary anaesthetic,' snapped Jicaque. 'This is the work of the codechanters.'

Blood pulled a face. 'The who?'

'I sense the nature of the rituals, the energy that lingers about him.' The old Native American nodded grimly. 'I should have expected as much.'

'Here we go with the mystical wise man act,' muttered Stacy.

'These codechanters … they're old men? Blind?' Sunday looked at Kate. 'German, maybe?'

He looked at her. 'You've encountered them?'

'One of them controlled my body just by speaking. He seemed to be training others, using me as some kind of guinea pig.'

'And two of his friends turned 'wolf and tried to kill us,' Kate said.

Jicaque nodded gravely. 'The codechanters are among the oldest of the European necromantic cults. They may be blind now, but those men have seen the threads that bind the body together. The strongest codechanters can undo those threads, or retie them in any way they choose.'

'Just by speaking?' Stacy looked sceptical, and Kate had to agree it sounded fantastic.

'If it would help, think of those threads as protein chains, as strands of DNA,' said Jicaque, pronouncing the letters as if they were distasteful to him. 'And think of the words the codechanters speak as a kind of hypnosis, an autosuggestion that affects all the ancient, untapped regions of the human mind. It releases certain chemicals in the brain, blocks the impulses of certain nerve endings, depending on the code spoken.'

'It's true,' said Sunday. 'I've felt it.'

'And so have I,' croaked Tom, struggling to rise from the bed. Stacy carefully propped up his head with a pillow. 'This old blind guy – Liebermann, they called him – he paralysed me. But I think he was going to do a lot more than that to the security guard Araminta Black took there,' he murmured.

Kate nodded grimly. 'He did.'

'Karl Liebermann,' breathed Jicaque. He looked troubled. 'It is as I thought. He is the most powerful of these men. Only he could control the nervous system with such skill.'

Blood raised a finger like a bewildered pupil seeking the teacher's help. 'Karl Liebermann?'

Jicaque glanced at him. 'He took control of the codechanters in the mid-nineteenth century.'

'He's over one hundred and fifty years old?' spluttered Stacy.

'He looks it,' Tom said, closing his eyes again.

'Those Jedi types in Tibet – yogis,' said Blood,

thoughtfully. 'They're meant to live to great ages, aren't they? Lower their heart rates, control wear and tear on the body …'

Jicaque nodded. 'It is a similar discipline. But as Tom and Sunday have experienced, the codechanters can turn this power on others.' He paused. 'Liebermann's mistake was to ally his cult with the Nazis in the 1930s. He used his powers in terrible experiments on humans and lupines alike, trying to breed werewolf supersoldiers to bolster the German forces.'

'I can see why Takapa would want to know these guys,' Kate said, uneasily.

'I had assumed they would be dead by now,' said Jicaque. 'When the Nazis fell from power, the new lupine regime turned on the codechanters. Liebermann and his followers were blinded as punishment for their experiments on the lupine race. Sympathisers helped them flee to South America.'

'But Takapa's found them,' Tom said weakly. 'And he's brought them out of retirement.'

Sunday stared at Kate. 'And to show he values them, he puts them in the penthouse at Brook Mansion,' she breathed. 'That heat, the fake foliage on the walls …'

'That South American touch,' Kate nodded. 'A regular home from home.'

'So, to summarise,' said Blood dryly, 'we have a new twist on the three blind mice – this lot can talk the farmer's wife to death.'

Stacy looked sharply at Blood as if hoping for an ally. 'Do you believe this stuff? Old men altering a body's biochemistry with *words*?'

'Well …' Blood looked at her apologetically. 'It

would explain that old myth of magic spells, wouldn't it? I mean, witches turning men into frogs – that would mean altering DNA, wouldn't it?'

She frowned. 'So, what, you believe in witches too?'

'No choice, love,' he grinned. 'I've dated enough of them!'

'The thing is,' Tom said, gingerly raising himself up on his elbows, 'what are they doing here?' He looked at Kate with bloodshot eyes. 'I saw Liebermann with your mom and dad, and Dr Walker. They were talking about regenerating the flesh of that König Man thing, the body from the peat bog.'

Kate shuddered. 'But its skin is mummified ... like leather or something.'

Jicaque rose from the bed and stared hard at her. 'You've seen the body?'

'We both have,' said Blood. 'It's at the gallery ready for the purebloods to view it tomorrow.'

'Regenerating the ancient skin and bone,' breathed the untidy old man, sinking back down on to the bed. 'That corpse has lain dormant for more than three hundred and seventy years, and now there's so little time.'

'What are you saying?' asked Sunday.

Jicaque looked at each of them in turn. 'Takapa is a revolutionary, yes? A 'wolf idealist, tired of his kind being forced to skulk in the shadows for fear of incurring the open wrath of humanity.'

Kate nodded. 'Sure. So he uses genetics to help the 'wolves evolve to a higher level – and to hit back at humans.'

Jicaque sighed and nodded. 'And he seeks to convince the purebloods that, if the 'wolf race is to flourish, it must unite under one strong leader.'

Blood snorted. 'What, and he really thinks he's a suitable candidate?'

'That is the crux of his work here in Chicago,' said Jicaque. 'He has shown himself to be fallible. In New Orleans, he was frustrated, and again in New York. He has lost face, and he knows it. So what he needs is a figurehead. An indisputable champion for whom the lupine race will rally together without question.'

'Who?' chimed in Tom. 'Surely that's the whole problem – there's no such person.'

'No living person, perhaps,' said Jicaque darkly. 'And so with his modern science, and with the necromantic arts of the codechanters, he has widened his scope.' His amber eyes were clouded with concern. 'He seeks to wrest life from the dead.'

Kate felt a long, creeping tingle down her spine. 'The body from the peat bog?'

'König Man,' breathed Blood.

'Yes, König.' Jicaque scowled. 'It means the king, the crowned man. And I believe the body to be that of a man of great evil. A man tortured to death in 1632 after a show trial, his evil, broken body dumped in wasteland without blessing or burial, for scavengers to devour. But I've heard tell that his followers retrieved the corpse in secret. Bound its shattered bones in healing ritual and dark prayer. Gave it up at last to the thick, squalid waters of the Gottenheim marshes, where it lay, preserved in blackness and silence.'

'How about you cut to the chase,' said Stacy dryly, though Kate noticed everyone else seemed spellbound.

'Centuries later, some expert – a scientist, a

palaeontologist, I don't know – stumbled upon this extraordinary find in the ancient, boggy ground. They lovingly unearthed him, imagined a past for him, scoured him and studied him, and when they had learned all they could, they put him on display.' Jicaque sighed. 'How could they know the dangers? To them he was just a man. But to the 'wolves ... to the secret historians ...'

'Who was this guy?' asked Tom.

'His name was Peter Stubbe,' said Jicaque slowly, as if he could barely bring himself to say the words out loud. 'Also known as the Great Wolf. Alleged to be the first werewolf in all Europe. His followers, the men and the women he turned against their own kind, took up his cause – went on to spread the plague of the 'wolf throughout the rest of Europe and on to America.'

'Stubbe,' Kate echoed, suddenly chilled to the bone. She knew about him in the same way normal families knew about Abraham Lincoln or JFK; Stubbe was the founding father of modern lupine society. Werewolf lore was peppered with his name. 'Of course ... he was sentenced to death in the seventeenth century on charges of murder and witchcraft.' She looked at Blood. 'That weird presence I felt at the gallery. It was *him*, Blood, I know it!'

Jicaque gave a grim smile. 'Clearly some remnant of Stubbe's evil soul has survived within his shrivelled remains ... Perhaps he sensed the wolf that waits within you.'

'So this is Project Resurrection,' breathed Tom.

Blood slapped a palm against his forehead. 'That must be why he's showing it off on Christmas Day. A sick kind of publicity stunt, if this is a kind of lupine second coming.'

'Shouldn't he have waited till Easter?' enquired Stacy dourly. 'That's the traditional time for a resurrection.'

'Lacks the same impact,' Blood pointed out. 'And can you see Takapa twiddling his thumbs for four months until April rolls around?'

'But why take the white wolves?' Kate asked.

Tom's eyes flickered back open. 'Dr Walker said something about combining wolf and human genes ... it was stuff he took from the wolves that was fixing up the corpse's skin.'

'Right,' said Sunday. 'As well as the decay of the skin and bone, with DNA that old, there'd surely be gaps in his genome – faulty genes affecting both human and 'wolf. And those white wolves are rare, right? Good-quality stock, breeding in isolated pockets ...'

Blood smiled faintly. 'Like darning his old socks with purest silk.'

'And Takapa will make this resurrection happen tomorrow,' Kate realised, horrified. 'That's what this pureblood gathering is here to see.'

'Like any other politician,' conceded Stacy. 'Get a celebrity endorsement to sex up your campaign.'

Tom nodded. 'That's what's going to get Takapa the support he needs.'

Jicaque inclined his head. 'So it would seem. Tomorrow, Peter Stubbe shall be given new life.'

'Das Zeitalter des Werwolfs,' Kate said, 'that old legend ...'

'The Time of the Werewolf,' Tom translated.

Kate bit her lip. 'Looks like it's starting.'

CHAPTER TWELVE

Jicaque took Tom into the other bedroom and spent what seemed like an age just chanting ancient texts and applying pressure to different points on his face and neck. In the rooms beyond, Tom could hear the sound of hasty packing. Blood wanted them to move out as soon as possible; it might not be safe for them here any longer.

'Your nervous system still holds the scars of the codechanters' assault,' Jicaque explained. 'I hope I can heal the damage.'

'Not as much as I do,' sighed Tom. 'How'd you learn this stuff? Is it Shipapi knowledge?' Tom knew that Jicaque was descended from an ancient order of missionaries, pledged to defend humanity from were-wolf predators. They took their weird name from an old Pueblo word, meaning *womb of the earth*, the place from which the first humans entered the world.

'The incantations are obscure, even for one of the Shipapi,' said Jicaque, smiling faintly. 'Lucky for you I've been cramming, absorbing all the ancient knowledge I can, in anticipation of my final battle.'

Tom frowned. 'Final battle?'

Jicaque took his old, leathery fingers from Tom's temples and looked at him, thoughtfully. 'The Shipapi knew of Stubbe, Tom. When the first Dutch colonies were founded in America in 1624, they brought with them word of 'wolves at work in Europe. Shipapi missionaries were dispatched there to bring those 'wolves to heel.'

'So what went wrong?' Tom murmured.

'The missionaries failed.' He laughed mirthlessly. 'They saw Stubbe executed, but his followers eluded them. If, indeed, they ever seriously tried to fulfil their sacred duty, for it would seem they were not strong men.'

Tom looked at the old medicine man. 'How'd you know so much about this?'

'I am descended directly from one of those missionaries,' said Jicaque. 'And I too have been guilty of neglecting my sacred trust, of letting lupine evil fester and grow.'

'You've made up for it since I've known you,' Tom assured him. 'You stopped Takapa in New York, you cured those poor people he turned 'wolf ...'

'Yes, I cured them,' agreed the old Native American. 'But I *could* have prevented their nightmare becoming a reality. I resolve to do so now, or to die trying.' A slow smile stretched his leathery skin. 'Though in truth, I am not a brave man, and would rather live forever if at all possible.'

Tom grinned. 'I'm with you on that one.'

'Then dress yourself, get packed, and we shall move on to safer quarters,' said Jicaque.

Kate was relieved to see Tom looking, if not the picture of health, then at least a rough cartoon of it. Even Stacy seemed impressed with the change in him, though of course she would never give Jicaque the credit.

'Good thing I brought the car here,' said Sunday as they bundled into the elevator together. 'Be a bit of a squeeze, six of us in Blood's car.'

'Nothing wrong with the odd bit of squeezing,' Blood observed, glancing slyly down at Stacy.

Sunday noticed, and smiled. She was looking a little better for a half-hour spent lying down with a cold cloth over her eyes.

The elevator didn't stop on the way down to the hotel reception. While Blood checked out, Kate caught herself wondering what Tom made of Sunday – full of curves, whereas Kate was just plain straight. *Nice going,* she told herself wryly. *The end of the world might start tomorrow and you're worrying if Tom's a breast man.* Who could blame him for going after Sunday? Wouldn't that be simpler, cleaner, better for everyone?

Tom glanced over, saw her watching him and smiled.

No, she decided, smiling back. It damn well wouldn't.

'So do we have any plan at all as to what to do next?' Tom asked.

Stacy shrugged. 'I heard some pretty fantastic stuff up in that room. But I work better with evidence.'

Kate was struck by a sudden realisation. 'Maybe I can help you out.' She reached into her pants pocket and produced the phial she'd taken from the operating room at the warehouse.

'What's this?' asked Stacy, peering at the grey detritus gathered at the bottom of the glass.

'I think they're skin samples. They might be from Stubbe's body,' Kate said, and explained how she'd come by them.

'Weird sciencey stuff, huh? Well, I guess that's why I'm here,' said Stacy wryly. 'An old colleague of mine works in a lab near Grand Avenue. Immunologist, so our interests kind of overlap. I'll look her up, see if she'll let me borrow a test-tube or two ...'

As Stacy went to call her friend, Sunday sighed. 'Guess we should've taken some of that stuff in the wheelchair for study too. Before my dad ate it all.'

'I was trying to forget about that,' Kate shuddered. 'What the hell did they *do* to that security guard?'

'Whatever it was, Liebermann was responsible,' Tom said. 'That's what was in store for Sunday. They drugged the guard so they could experiment on him instead of her. It seemed important to get it right.'

'Describe the remains that you saw,' said Jicaque urgently.

'It was just ... a kind of mush,' Kate told him. 'Like every bit of the guy had decomposed to next to nothing.'

'The guy looked OK when they wheeled him in last night,' Tom said.

Jicaque nodded, still fixing Kate with his amber eyes. 'As if the binding force of his body, the *soul* ... had been removed?'

'If that would leave him looking like security-guard puree,' Kate said uncertainly, 'then maybe.'

'I think you're right, Jicaque.' Sunday looked spooked. 'That ceremony Liebermann was performing on me, before Tom came crashing in ... I felt like I was coming undone from the inside.'

'Good thing Stacy's not hearing this,' Kate observed, watching her talking animatedly on the phone. 'You're saying these codechanters can separate a soul from a living body – like a dentist pulls a tooth?'

Jicaque nodded. 'The soul is just one name for the psychic energy held within our minds and bodies.' His eyes narrowed. 'They have Stubbe's body back from that peat bog – and can restore his withered flesh with certainty. But the mind and soul ...' He glanced at Stacy, just finishing her call. 'That requires more than mere science – it requires art. It seems they are planning to use a donor's psychic energy to refresh the remnants left in Stubbe's body. If they succeed, they will have achieved the ultimate resurrection.'

'I think I've just achieved the ultimate hotel bill, if anyone's interested,' said Blood, tucking his wallet back into his jacket pocket. 'Come on, let's go. I'm feeling slightly faint.'

'I'm going to that lab,' said Stacy proudly, pocketing the phone and shaking the phial. 'It closes at twelve for the holidays, but my friend says I can stay on as long as I need.'

'We don't *have* long,' muttered Sunday.

'If the body's at the gallery,' Tom said, 'why don't we just ... I don't know – torch it or something? Turn Stubbe into toast?'

Jicaque smiled sadly. 'How would we be certain of his destruction? Do you not think the 'wolves would sacrifice *anything* to preserve such a prize?'

Tom wasn't ready to give up. 'Well, couldn't we phone 911, say there's a bomb in there or something, just as the whole thing's about to start?'

140

Blood looked sceptical. 'That might delay them for a few hours ... then what?'

'So, what *do* we do?' asked Sunday.

'I must finish what my ancestor started,' said Jicaque, 'all those centuries ago. I must confront Stubbe and try to end this madness.'

'Uh-oh,' Sunday announced, stiffening. 'Trouble's coming.'

Kate turned to find Mike sprinting through the parking lot towards them. 'What does *he* want?'

Mike staggered to a stop in front of them, red-faced with exertion. 'I know where they've taken Fayn and Chung,' he blurted.

'We can rest easy again, chaps,' said Blood wryly.

'Some place in Oak Brook,' panted Mike.

Kate frowned. 'Brook Mansion?'

Mike nodded, still catching his breath. 'They're forcing Chung to tell the purebloods he's on Takapa's side. Help win them over. Or else they kill Fayn.'

'How do you know all this?' Kate demanded.

'The Chapter has contacts all over, remember? I asked around, got a lead. Some jerk-off in Uptown, a guy who never showed at the yard this morning ... turns out he's real tight with a 'wolf in Takapa's crew.'

'So *he* told Takapa you were coming?' asked Tom.

Mike shook his head. 'Don't think so. I laid into him pretty hard. He was scared to death, but he didn't 'fess up.'

'What a sweet little "enforcer" you are,' said Blood mildly.

'So, what,' said Sunday, 'you're expecting us to go charging off to rescue your pals?'

For a moment, Mike looked abashed. Then his face

hardened over. 'All I want from you people is a fast, free ride out there. I can do the rest by myself.'

'You're going to get inside and rescue Chung and Fayn single-handed?' Kate shook her head. 'Take it from one who's been there – I don't think so.'

'Wait,' Tom said. 'Araminta said the purebloods were arriving there at noon, ready for …' He struggled to remember the exact words. 'For a preliminary briefing.'

'Takapa spouting some PR bullshit, I expect,' said Blood. 'So?'

'Well, if everyone's busy at this meeting, we might stand a better chance of finding Chung.'

Sunday scowled. 'And why would we want to do that?'

'Chung's name is a big deal to the purebloods, right?' Tom argued. 'If we can keep Chung from swearing support for Takapa's plans, Takapa would be shown up … it might even weaken his standing.'

'You're grasping at straws, hon,' said Stacy sadly.

Tom threw up his hands. 'What else can we do? Sit and watch while you stare at a few scraps of skin through a microscope? This whole thing kicks off at midnight!'

'I agree,' Kate said. She'd decided, whatever was going to happen, she would face it with Tom there. 'Anyone else?'

Jicaque shook his head. 'It is with Stubbe that I must do battle, not his acolytes. I must prepare for that confrontation. Will someone take me to this gallery that houses him?'

'I will,' sighed Blood. 'Suppose it makes sense – if we're going to get in there again, we need to know how security's improved since the old guard's been replaced.'

Sunday looked a little shyly at Stacy. 'Need a lab assistant? I helped out my dad sometimes.'

Stacy slipped an arm round her. 'I thought no one was going to offer. Let's get going.'

'I'll drop you and Sunday off at this lab, then go on to the Bane Gallery with Jicaque,' said Blood.

Stacy scribbled down the address of the lab and gave it to Tom. 'In case you need me.'

'Oh, and Tom, Kate ...' Blood looked kind of embarrassed. 'Take care, all right?'

'And take my car,' Sunday told Kate, handing her the keys.

'Let's get going,' Mike urged them.

'One thing,' said Jicaque gravely. 'Remember, the 'wolves have taken what they need from you now, Tom. If they capture you again, they will kill you.'

Tom nodded slowly. 'And on that bright and cheery note ...' he said. Amid the chorus of farewells he got into the passenger seat beside Kate while Mike clambered into the back.

'What the hell have we let ourselves in for?' sighed Tom.

Kate started the engine, took a deep breath and stepped on the gas.

The journey was slowed by heavy traffic, as the whole of Chicago seemed set on getting home for the afternoon. Tom tried to keep himself calm, to save his energy for the inevitable nightmare that lay ahead. The 'wolf in him was hungry for release; he had that familiar feeling of twitching on the inside, an unsettling tickle that only claws could scratch.

No way, Tom vowed. *I'm stronger than you. I will not give in to you.*

Kate drove them through the swanky suburban neighbourhood and down a driveway she said led to Brook Mansion.

'Here goes nothing,' muttered Mike.

The old Chrysler growled along the driveway. As the main gates came into sight, Tom saw the two men who leaned against them stiffen to attention.

Kate wound down the window and offered them the slightly battered invitation Blood had given her. A ferret-faced man in a trenchcoat, his thinning hair slicked back, took the invitation dubiously. He studied it, then turned to his friend and shrugged. The friend pulled a radio from his black jacket and spoke into it. Seconds later, the gate opened with an angry buzz.

'Go through to the main building,' said Mr Slick. 'You'll be met there for a full ID check against the register.' He leaned in through the window, peering uncertainly at Tom. Then a spark of recognition sparked in his grey eyes. 'Hey, wait a minute. You're—'

Mike rose up from his crouching position beneath a blanket in the back and jabbed a needle into the man's hand. Tom almost sympathised as the guy's eyes glazed over and he slumped to the ground; Mike had hit Tom with the same thing when the Dark Chapter had collared him outside Takapa's.

'That's the thing with this city,' muttered Mike, with a fleeting smile. 'Never know when you might find trouble.'

The man in the black jacket was coming over to see what was wrong. Tom flung open the car door, which swung into the guard's midriff and sent him sprawling. As he struggled to get up, Tom punched him hard in the jaw, swearing as he jarred his fist in the process. The man stayed down.

'Take his radio,' Kate said. 'Mike, help him get those bodies out of sight!'

Mike nodded and scrambled out of the car.

With the bodies hidden in the undergrowth, Tom and Mike got back in the car.

'Better call ahead, put them on the wrong track,' said Kate, flashing Tom a nervous smile as she drove smoothly through the gates. 'Unless you like the sound of that full ID check.'

Tom studied the radio briefly, then hit the talk button. 'This is main gate,' he said, roughening his voice. 'Intruders sighted around the back of the building. Moving fast. Repeat, around the back. Get going.' He shrugged at Kate. 'They may fall for it.'

'They'd better,' said Mike. 'I've only got one more needle left.'

'Whatever.' Kate stepped on the gas a little. 'For better or worse, we're in.'

Behind them, the gate buzzed slowly shut.

CHAPTER THIRTEEN

There was no one to meet them when they pulled up outside the hotel. Tom cautiously got out of the car. Scuffed footprints in the fine gravel on the drive suggested someone had taken off in a hurry – there were no guards.

'Come on,' Kate said, running over to the entrance. 'Inside!'

The reception area was empty. Mike looked around suspiciously, then turned to Kate and Tom. 'That trick with the radio won't have bought us much time. What do we do?'

'There's some kind of conference room on the next floor,' said Kate, hesitantly climbing the stairs. 'If everyone's at this briefing Tom mentioned, we might have a better chance to look around—'

'And get Chung and Fayn out of here,' concluded Mike.

Once they'd scaled the stairs, Tom followed Kate and Mike down the long corridor. The sound of a woman's voice carried from a nearby room. Carefully, he peered through the narrow viewing panel in the door to the conference room. 'We're in luck,' he said grimly.

Araminta Black was standing at a lectern, speaking to an audience of about fifty people.

'Too bad I didn't slug her harder,' Tom muttered.

'Or that Sunday's dad didn't eat her alive,' added Kate.

Behind Araminta sat Marcie Folan, her face sallow and grave, and Liebermann with the two other creepy old men. But there was no sign of Chung and, more disturbingly, no sign of Takapa. Maybe he was with Stubbe right now. Maybe the two of them were working out their lines for that night's performance ...

'... The acid in the *schwarztorf*, the darker peaty layers, had prevented the body from decaying,' Araminta was explaining, 'along with the lack of oxygen beneath the bog's surface. The corpse looked only recently buried, and the farmers who made the discovery in 1994 had no idea of the true value of their find. The scientific community expressed a polite interest, but the body was far more recent than those Iron Age individuals dredged up from the depths in Northern Europe, and so of limited interest. For years, the man's body languished in laboratory vaults, wheeled out now and then so that dutiful specialists could defile his aged flesh with their futile experiments ...'

'What are we hanging around for?' hissed Mike. 'Who needs a lecture? Let's get going.'

Kate shushed him furiously. 'I'm trying to see how far in to the story she's got – how long we may have.'

'... Finally, the body of this man was taken back to Gottenheim and displayed in a provincial museum for schoolchildren to coo at,' said Araminta, her skinny features twisted in disgust. 'But by then, I had formulated my own ideas as to who this man might truly be. I researched patiently, diligently ... and as curator of the Bane Gallery, I was eventually granted a private view.' She paused impressively. 'My suspicions were confirmed. *I* was right. *I* had found *him*. And I knew then, I must secure the body for myself.' She glanced back nervously at Marcie. 'So that, naturally, we *all* might benefit ...'

'All right,' Kate said, 'she's on a real ego trip. This could run and run. Come on.'

Tom risked one last glimpse through the window in the door. There was everyone sitting nice and comfy in their regimented lines, attentive to Araminta as she spoke.

Only Liebermann's head was cocked to one side, his ruined, sightless eyes trained on the door. Seeming to look straight at Tom, the tiniest hint of a smile on his ancient, lined face.

Mike must've noticed it too. 'It's all right,' he said as they crept away. 'The guy's blind.'

'I know,' Tom said as they walked away from the conference room, but he felt no better.

All three of them jumped as the radio in Tom's pocket suddenly squawked into life. He grabbed hold of it, fumbled for the talk button.

'Main gate?' came a man's voice, sparking with static. 'Entrance here. No sign of intruders.'

'If that had gone off outside the door ...' muttered Kate, her cheeks reddening.

Tom held up the radio to his lips. 'Uh ... well they didn't come back this way.'

'Do you have a description?' barked the radio.

'Yes,' blurted Tom, suddenly seized by inspiration. 'One of them was an Asian male, about twenty.'

'The Dark Chapter leader?' came the crackling

response. 'But he was tied up nice and tight in the penthouse.'

Tom raised his fist in a victory salute, and Mike almost cried out with delight. Kate grabbed Tom's arm, excited, as he went on. 'Other intruder was older male, brown hair and a squint.'

There was a pause, then again the radio squawked. 'The other Chapter guy? Ain't he on our side?'

The grin froze on Mike's face. Kate's hand flew to her mouth, and Tom felt a chill crawl along the back of his neck.

Another burst of static. 'Main gate? You receiving?'

'Uh … just keep looking, they can't have got far,' Tom said weakly. 'Out.' He let the radio slip from his hands to the soft carpet.

'So now we know how Takapa found out our plans,' said Mike, his face darkening.

'Never mind him now,' snapped Kate. 'That guy said Chung was in the penthouse. That's on the next floor.' She led the way to the next flight of stairs. 'Let's move – before school finishes for the day.'

Kate's heart was racing as she reached the second floor and the sinister oak door in the long white wall. The memory of the penthouse kept pinching the back of her mind, making her want to run outside screaming.

'It's through there,' she told Tom.

'This is where our three blind mice like to hang out?'

'And trust me,' she said, 'you've never seen a hole in the wall like this one.'

Mike strode past them and threw open the door.

A familiar prickling wave of heat swept over Kate. The place was much as she'd left it before – a deranged jungle of textures and shapes – except that the lights were back on. Regardless, from the look on Tom's face, Kate could tell that he was just as freaked out as she'd been.

'Jeez,' croaked Mike.

Kate suddenly noticed Chung, lying on his back in the ball pool.

Mike made his way there at once, dodging past the chairs and statues that littered the mosaic floor. He waded into the plastic pond and lifted Chung out.

'He's breathing!' he called, setting him down in a hard-backed chair beside a small fountain. 'He's going to be OK.'

Kate looked at Chung and hoped Mike was right. His face and neck were bruised and swollen. 'Whatever they wanted him to do, looks like he put up a fight.'

Tom shushed her. 'I heard something,' he whispered, pointing to the middle one of the three doors set into the far wall of the room.

He crept towards it, Kate just behind him. Mike left Chung slumped in the chair and followed them.

Tom threw open the door – and Fayn jumped back in surprise. He'd obviously been pressing his sweaty face up against the wood, listening. Mixed with the tang of fear, Tom picked up a faint but familiar lupine scent from Fayn – that of the 'wolf he'd fought at the zoo.

Fayn retreated into the small, simple bedroom, decorated in the same style as those downstairs but as hot as hell. He stared at each of them in turn, his squint more pronounced than ever. 'Thank God, you found me!' he said, grabbing his discarded leather jacket from the floor and bundling it up in both hands. 'I thought I'd never get out.'

'The door wasn't locked, Russ,' said Mike coldly. 'So what're you doing in here? You like the wallpaper or something?'

Fayn looked deeply rattled. 'Takapa ... he had his people bring us here – me and Chung. They did something to him, man! He's unconscious – I couldn't just leave him, could I?'

Mike clenched his fists. 'And that's why they left the door unlocked?'

'I guess.' Fayn looked uneasily at Tom and Kate, bunching up the jacket in both hands like a security blanket. 'I mean, no one can get out of this building anyway ...'

'Don't feed me that crap,' thundered Mike, grabbing hold of Fayn by his shoulders and slamming him up against the wall. 'I'll tell you why they never locked that door. Because they've hurt Chung so bad he's in no state to go anywhere, plus they've got you here to watch over him – and you don't *want* to get out of here!'

'You're crazy, Mike!' shouted Fayn.

'We know you sold us out. You got Zac killed.'

'No!' Fayn struggled against Mike's grip. 'It wasn't like that—'

'Oh? Then how the hell *was* it?'

Kate shifted uneasily, glancing back towards the main door. 'Mike, we don't have time for this.'

Mike didn't seem to hear her. 'You're *Chapter*, Russ!' he bawled, tearing the wolf's head brooch from

151

Fayn's jacket. 'The Chapter comes first, remember? Doesn't this mean anything to you, *pureblood* Fayn?'

Fayn stared at the brooch, his face gradually changing from protesting innocence to angry sneer. 'Sure it means something. It means *Chung's* family. His goddamned ancestors setting up the whole show, lording it over the rest of us.' He let his jacket fall heavily to the floor. 'Chung doesn't care about *us*, Mike! This is just about him and his ego, living up to the past! He doesn't give a damn that *my* family have got a name, that *we've* been watching over Chicago too since—'

Mike gripped him by the throat, choked off the words. 'What, so you sold us out because you got a chip on your shoulder?'

'They told Chung they'd kill me if he didn't speak up for Takapa,' gasped Fayn. 'Chung didn't know it was just talk, but it made no difference. He wouldn't do it. Oh, and do you want to know what's funny? He said I'd understand! Thought I'd die a happy pureblood knowing he was keeping our goddamned honour.'

'That's the difference between just having a name, and making it mean something,' hissed Mike. 'Chung isn't a whining hypocrite like you.'

Fayn shook his head. 'All Chung cares about is the past. But Takapa ... he cares about the future. Big changes are coming, Mike. If you don't get behind Takapa, man, you're going to get left behind. A dinosaur. Just a name that doesn't mean a thing. Like Chung's going to be, once Takapa's through with him.'

Tom marched up to Mike. 'That's enough. Kate's right, we don't have time for this.'

Kate nodded. 'We've got to get Chung out of here, fast.'

Mike stared hatefully at Fayn. Then he brought up his knee hard into the man's groin and smashed down his fist on the back of his neck. Fayn crumpled to the foor.

'I should kill him for this,' Mike said thickly.

'That's not going to bring anyone back,' Tom said, 'and it could get us caught.'

'So let's grab your friend and go,' Kate agreed.

'You wouldn't be thinking of leaving us so soon, surely?' came a low, brittle voice from outside the room.

Kate turned, bile rising in her throat. Liebermann's stooped and sinister figure was framed in the doorway.

'I thought I heard visitors come calling,' he explained, a yellow-toothed smile deepening the cracks in his ancient face. 'So I crept away to check, as quiet as a mouse. As a *blind* mouse, you could say, yes? But your scent guided me as easily as eyes.'

But while Tom just stared and Kate stood fixed in fright, Mike was still fired up. He pulled out his last hypodermic syringe and threw himself at Liebermann. The needle pushed into the leathery folds of the old man's neck.

Mike staggered back, watching and waiting for Liebermann to go down.

But the old man only muttered under his breath, cocked his head to one side. 'Home brew?' He chuckled and licked his lips. 'Yes ... a compound of ligno-caine and morphine, I believe.'

He's holding back the effect, Kate realised, *with*

nothing more than the power of his mind.

'Yes,' Liebermann continued, 'such a mixture would have a considerable anaesthetic effect on most victims … but not on me.' Suddenly his elderly fist shot out like a hydraulic ram into Mike's throat.

Mike crashed backwards into the wall. Kate saw his startled face turn crimson, heard the sound of frothing fluid as he struggled to draw breath through his crushed windpipe.

Tom crouched to try and help Mike, and Liebermann started to chant his dark code.

Kate shrieked at the top of her lungs.

The old man winced, clutched at his ears, then swung around to face her. 'Sorry, my dear,' he cackled mirthlessly. 'I'm afraid that trick won't help you against me.' He started to chant again.

In his hand, Kate saw his disconnected hearing aid. She felt a crushing wave of coldness break through her body.

Then there came the sound of broken glass from the main room, and the crazed tinkling of a disturbed windchime. She and Tom both looked up, startled.

Liebermann must have heard it too, however faintly. He paused, cocked his head.

Taking advantage of the distraction, Tom threw himself at the old man. His momentum carried them both into the main room, where they collapsed flailing to the floor.

Kate stumbled forwards to see what was happening and almost fell, her legs numb and unresponsive.

Chung stood swaying in the ball pool next to a broken window. Whether by accident or design, he'd knocked over a heavy brass statue that had smashed through the glass. He staggered over to try and help Tom, who was struggling on the floor with the livid Liebermann.

Kate looked around for an object she could use as a weapon. Maybe Mike was carrying something? She crossed unsteadily back to the bedroom, where he was now lying slumped on the floor beside the unconscious Fayn, beetroot-faced and no longer breathing. His eyes were wide open and as sightless as Liebermann's. Fresh fear now mingled with her shock and pity – no old man had Liebermann's supernatural strength. Then she thought of martial arts, the way adepts focused the mind to harden the flesh, smashing through bricks with their bare hands – a child's trick, surely, for a master of mind over matter, regardless of how old and infirm he might appear.

In desperation she grabbed Fayn's discarded leather jacket, hoping she could throw the heavy fabric over Liebermann's head to distract him. But as she ran back out into the main room she saw she was too late. Liebermann had hurled Tom towards an abstract stone sculpture, and he struck it with a sick thud.

The old man was back on his feet, speaking his code in that hoarse, creepy monotone. Again, Kate felt dizzy and cold, but Chung rushed him, a length of plastic foliage held like a rope in both hands. He looped it around the old man's neck and pulled back hard. Liebermann tottered and fell into the ball pool.

Kate started instinctively towards Tom, to check he was all right.

'Help me!' yelled Chung.

Kate's heart leaped as she saw what he was doing.

He was jamming one of the plastic balls into Liebermann's dribbling mouth, stifling the flow of words. 'Swallow that, you old bastard.'

'What he can't say can't hurt us,' Kate agreed. Her arms cramped and aching, she hurled the leather jacket over Liebermann's head, muffling his gagging noises as he tried to spit out the ball. The old man's bony fingers flapped and scrabbled at the heavy fabric, trying to tear it clear.

Chung sunk to his knees, gasping with exertion as Liebermann flailed about. 'Must rest,' he muttered, pulling his leathers tight around him like he was cold. 'Just for a minute. Then we've got to get out of here.'

For a few moments Kate stood staring. A part of her, deep inside, felt grey and old and numb.

Violence. Death. All around us.

Kate turned and ran on her stiff legs to see if Tom was all right.

It reaches closer and deeper all the time.

She shouted his name. He was writhing on the floor, shaking.

Always all around us.

As she reached him she saw the fury in his face, saw the muscles bunching in his arms and legs. 'Tom, no!' she hissed.

He was changing. Kate watched his strong, straight features lengthen and twist, like seeing his reflection in a fairground hall of mirrors. She saw the claws curve out of his fingers, the dark hair coiling from out of his smooth skin.

The memory of the nightmare she'd had that first night at the Drake came flooding back – of the two of them in the dark together, in each other's arms, Tom's 'wolf rising up and tearing through her ...

Violence and death. We run and run but we never escape it.

Liebermann's half-spoken words were still trapped in her head. Her legs were so stiff now she could barely feel them.

So she fell to her knees and held Tom just as tight as she could.

His bones cracked dully like glass in a fire. His jaw lengthened, his snout trailed cold slime down her cheek. Saliva drenched her hair and neck, mingled with her sweat. He could bite through her throat in a moment without even meaning to, an instinctive snap in the throes of the change. She could die here, cradling his sleek, animal form. Or the bite could change her for ever, set free the lupine that prowled her blackest nightmares. As a pureblood there could be no cure, no going back for her ...

But for that long trusting moment while she held him, none of that mattered.

The change was complete now. Tom shook softly, holding himself quite still in her arms. She felt the muscles in his flank shiver beneath her fingers, shifted on her knees and looked into the beast's dark eyes. *Tom's* eyes.

'We have to get out of here,' she whispered, wishing she could cry but finding nothing inside.

'Someone's coming!' Chung shouted.

Kate heard the main door creak open.

The two remaining blind mice scuttled into their penthouse.

Anton, the short, portly one, sniffed the air and nodded. 'It's the girl again,' he proclaimed.

Friedrich stooped to lock the door. 'I did wonder what was keeping Liebermann.'

'We can't have this.' Anton shook his head and tutted, his pride seemingly hurt. 'No, certainly not.'

Tom rounded on the old men, snapping his jaws, placing himself in front of Kate protectively.

Chung staggered over and helped her to her feet.

'Stop them,' croaked Liebermann behind them. He'd managed to get free of the jacket over his head.

Kate bunched her fists and faced up to the old men. 'You can't paralyse us like *he* can,' she insisted. 'If you could you'd have done it to me and Sunday before.'

'Even so,' said Anton, 'old 'wolves though we be, we are not entirely toothless.'

Kate opened her mouth ready to scream.

But Friedrich had already started chanting and now Anton took up the low, rasping incantation.

In seconds a fire had taken hold inside Kate's head. The searing pain drove all sense and words from her mind. The flames consumed her until nothing was left inside but darkness – the bitter, voiding darkness of an unhappy ending.

CHAPTER FOURTEEN

For Tom, the codechanters' verbal assault was like a hundred drums pounding inside his skull. He skittered back, knocking into Chung, who was slapping his bruised head with both hands like it was leaking and he didn't know how to plug the hole.

He saw Chung's eyes burn a fierce, pure yellow as his body reacted to his pain, his anger, and let slip the 'wolf.

Tom ran in circles like a deranged animal, smashing into statues, splintering chairs, tearing down foliage with his jaws. He saw Liebermann start to rise, knocked him back down without even meaning to, his body careering out of control.

Then he was at the broken window, gulping down cold air. He had to clear his head, had to go back and attack – rescue Kate. He could still feel her cool hands on him. He wanted her back; the cool hands, the sweet smell.

But then something slammed into him, knocked him through the window.

Chung, the 'wolf, wild and scrabbling for escape.

Tom landed on the gravelled roof of the porch two storeys below, scraping his shoulder. He rolled over and stared up at the window to the penthouse, hopelessly out of reach now. Chung lay beside him, still clothed in the tatters of his leather jacket, and Tom snapped at him, growled his aggression.

But the pain in his head was clearing.

The old men appeared at the window, peering out like they could see, their dry, fleshless faces scrunched up and furious.

Chung leaped down from the roof, and Tom followed him, the thought of the pain in his brain spurring him to flight. He hit the wet turf of the hotel gardens, trying to focus on the cold, earthy smells all around. He had to stay calm, had to think. Perhaps if they circled around, he could reach the penthouse again from the inside ...

He saw men out in the grounds, running for him and Chung. His own fault – hadn't he told those men that the intruders were out here? He saw that even as the guards ran, they were changing. In the blur of a few moments, they were 'wolves, eyes clear and cold, focused in pursuit.

Tom ran after Chung. He nuzzled open a door that led on to a glass and wood structure adjoining the main building. His mind groped for the manmade word – *conservatory*.

This conservatory was packed with bloody, half-chewed corpses. Most were young men, in torn black leathers. From the pain in Chung's eyes, Tom knew this must be the Dark Chapter's massacred attack force. But there were also two older men in the pile. Tom recognised their twisted, terrified faces. They were the scientists he'd found locked up at Takapa's lair. Their minds had been bled dry, but their bodies were still of use – as food. At least Sunday's father wasn't on the menu. Not today's menu, anyway.

'*They'll know some peace, soon enough*,' Marcie had said.

While Chung could only stare at the charnel offerings, Tom heard applause wash across from the hotel, enthusiastic human hands clapping. A voice rising over the clamour, and then swift and heavy animal footsteps thundering downstairs. Araminta's talk had finished, and in reward for the purebloods' patience, here was a free lunch.

Suddenly 'wolves were padding into the conservatory, scenting the meat and salivating. Tom herded Chung around the back of the pile of bodies as their pursuers burst in through the conservatory doors. But now the hungry purebloods were milling about, snapping at the buffet, a living, breathing barrier between hunters and hunted.

The guards barked and whined, trying to get to Tom and Chung. Tom's teeth closed on the back of Chung's tattered jacket and he dragged him away into the main building, pushing through the drooling throng who were focused only on the food.

When they reached the reception area, Tom broke away from Chung, intent on getting back up to the penthouse, to somehow get Kate back.

But the three blind men stood at the top of the stairs, blocking the way.

Tom's eyes narrowed. Perhaps if he moved fast enough he could kill all three, bite and break their scrawny necks ...

Not a chance.

As Liebermann opened his mouth to chant, Tom found himself bolting after Chung with a sick desperation to escape. Afraid and ashamed, and grieving.

The taxi driver hadn't wanted to make a fight of it; that was good. But then one guy against two slavering werewolves weren't terrific odds, Tom guessed. He'd fled his cab, screaming to the wide-open empty street about giant monsters. But the houses around here were set so far back from the road that Tom doubted anyone would hear him for blocks.

Tom and Chung had taken his idling cab and here they were, two naked men sitting in Christmas Eve traffic. Tom was driving. Chung was just sitting in sullen silence, cradling his ruined leather jacket in his lap and shaking his head in shock.

'We should never have left Kate,' Tom muttered for about the thirtieth time.

This time, Chung decided to reply. 'Her mom wants her alive, right? And so does that pink-eyed bastard, Takapa,' he said. 'Whereas you – they've got what they want from you. If you'd stayed, you'd have been killed. Wound up on the party platter, belly-up – the cherry on the cake.'

Tom could see the logic, but it made him feel no better. Even so, with all Chung had lost today he guessed maybe he should shut up. 'You know ... I'm sorry about—'

'Yeah,' Chung broke in. 'And Takapa's going to be, too.' He put his head in his hands. 'Shit, I still can't believe that Fayn would betray the Chapter.'

'Believe it,' Tom said coldly.

'He's pureblood, man. How could he disgrace his name?' He sighed. 'Guess it explains all that bull he gave us about how it was *you* helping to pull that white wolf stunt down at the zoo. He was trying to cover himself.'

Tom nodded. 'We had a lupine fight – I won, and took his place in the truck with the wolves. I recognised his lupine scent, back there in the penthouse.'

'You can bet your life,' said Chung, 'that just as soon as Fayn got hold of a change of clothes and a quarter for the phone, he was telling Takapa what you'd done.'

'Probably why Marcie and Lieberman came looking for me,' Tom agreed quietly. 'I suppose he *would* tell you guys I had a hand in it – he didn't think I'd make it out again to call him a liar.'

'Liar's just the tip of the iceberg,' muttered Chung.

They drove on slowly in silence till they were well into the city's heart. On one street, a frumpy-looking woman weighed down with bags struggled over to their cab with a hopeful look on her face. Tom swore – the traffic was gridlocked, he couldn't pull away. The woman leaned in to speak – then her mouth fell wide open as she saw that the cabbie and his passenger were completely nude. Shocked speechless, she turned around and tottered off back to the sidewalk.

Tom and Chung looked at each other for a few moments, then burst out laughing, almost hysterical. It helped them both, breaking some of the pent-up tensions inside.

Chung's smile faded as the moment passed and reality crept back in to stifle them. 'So where the hell do we go now?'

'To see Stacy at that lab,' Tom decided. 'I think I

remember the address. We can see if she's found anything out.'

'And see if she can get us some clothes,' Chung added dryly.

'Then we can give her and Sunday a ride over to the Bane Gallery,' Tom said. 'Get the lowdown from Blood and Jicaque.'

'I've heard of him. The old medicine man?'

'Uh-huh. He's our secret weapon against Takapa.'

'He'd better be,' said Chung. ''Cause it's no secret we need something on our side.'

'He's come through for us in the past.'

'And this Stubbe guy's come through for them *from* the past. So, Tom – which do *you* reckon is stronger?'

Tom thought of the resignation, the fear he'd seen in Jicaque's face, and realised he couldn't answer.

Three hours later, Tom sat beside Chung in a lab coat, waiting for cells to divide on a microscope slide and for Sunday to get back with some clothes. They'd dumped the taxi around the corner after a long and frustrating journey in circles trying to find the place. Chung had tied his jacket round his waist like a kind of kilt, but Tom'd had to settle for making leg holes in a plastic carrier bag discarded in the back, so he could at least cover something of his modesty before streaking barefoot to the laboratory.

Telling Sunday and Stacy the bad news about Kate while wearing improvised plastic pants had been a surreal experience to say the least. Then Stacy had sent Sunday off with some cash to try and find them some clothes.

She'd been busy in their absence. A line of three

benches in the large, spotless laboratory had been taken over with all kinds of clutter and printouts. Tinctures, solutions, pipettes and bottles and jars were ranged all around Stacy, together with slides and centrifuges and God-knew-what.

'The wonderful world of big-business immunology,' she observed. 'Oh, what it is to be financed. On the grants we get at my hospital ...'

'What are you actually doing?' asked Tom.

'Just running tests, playing a few hunches, you know,' said Stacy airily. 'I've got some pretty interesting results on these skin samples ...'

'Why do you even want to be involved in all this 'wolf stuff?' Chung asked her, surly and mistrustful.

'Pretty simple,' said Stacy, peering through a weird-looking microscope. 'In New York I saw first-hand how Takapa can hurt people. I want to do what I can to stop him.'

'What, so you're a Girl Guide?'

'I have my reasons. Now shut up and let me work, OK?'

'Just before we do,' Tom said, 'you have Blood's number, right?'

She tossed him her cell phone. 'It should be in there.'

Blood answered after a single ring. 'Adam Blood,' he said, smooth and cultivated. 'Is this the lovely Stacy?'

'Knock it off,' Tom told him.

'Anderson! What's been happening?'

'Nothing good,' Tom told him. 'We lost Kate.'

'Fornicating furies, how the frigging hell did that happen?'

'Those three blind mice again. Me and Chung got out, but Mike—'

'Spare me the gruesome details,' Blood interrupted. 'Things are bad enough as it is. Jicaque keeps going into some kind of trance, preparing himself for "the coming ordeal", as he likes to put it. Which is fine, but makes him lousy company.' He paused. 'You know, a grey limousine was parked outside the Bane Gallery when we got here.'

Tom felt a tingle in his guts. 'Takapa?'

'Yeah, bloody poser. That skinny cow who runs the place showed up a while back, and I think maybe Marcie Folan did too.'

'You think?'

'To be honest, I crouched down out of sight at the first inkling. People have been coming and going all afternoon. I don't know what they're up to in there, but Jicaque's not getting happy vibes off the place.'

Tom sighed. 'Does he think he can get inside?'

'We're working on that. Call us when you're ready to come and join. And we'll shout if there's any sign of Trolly this end.' He hung up.

As Tom placed the phone back on Stacy's adopted desk, Sunday came back holding a big bag. 'I had a spree at Old Navy,' she announced. 'Talk about last-minute shopping – they were dying to close up. Hope they fit.'

'Hallelujah,' Tom said, as with a smile she tossed him some blue jeans, a black hoodie and deck shoes. She dumped the bag and the rest of its contents at Chung's feet without a word.

'Thanks,' said Chung as he picked up the bag.

Sunday sat back next to Stacy. 'Thank her. She paid for it.'

Chung pulled on a pair of combat pants, and looked at her thoughtfully. 'Guess you must hate me pretty bad, huh?'

'What do you care?' asked Sunday, without turning around.

'Well?'

'What's to hate? Oh, aside from the fact that you were quite prepared to hand me over as raw 'wolf-meat to a stranger?' Her voice started to rise. 'Aside from the fact that creatures like you aren't content to turn my dad into a monster, you have to make him, like, some kind of junkie too—'

'I had nothing to do with that shit,' said Chung hotly. 'Don't try to make out I'm like Takapa.'

'Duh, hello!' Sunday shook her head in disbelief. 'You're both *werewolves*, aren't you?'

'Takapa's garbage. I hate him as much as you do.'

'Why?' yelled Sunday back at him. 'Because he turned your buddies into raw hamburger? Well, what have you and your buddies been doing to people like me your whole life, huh? Is it different when you actually *know* who's getting gnawed on? Or maybe you're just uptight 'cause it's werewolf eating werewolf – the superior beings snacking on each other instead of some crappy old human? Is that what's pissing you off, you goddamned hypocrite? Huh?'

Chung looked away. 'The Dark Chapter has always put limits on the kills in this city,' he said quietly. 'Without us a whole lot more humans would be dead.'

'Not because you care about life,' said Sunday.

'Only because you want to keep the heat off your own hairy back.'

'Hey, hon,' said Stacy quietly. 'You want to hate me along with our pureblood friend here? Because it was me who helped make your dad a junkie, not him. I developed that bloodlust drug they use.'

'Come on, Stacy,' Tom argued. 'You were making a serum you thought would help newbloods control their 'wolf urges. You were trying to *save* lives.'

'Sure. And Takapa took that ambition and twisted it around to serve his.' She pointed at Chung. 'So don't aim your hate at him. He never asked to be born a 'wolf. The hunt's in his blood, it's all he knows. That's not evil, that's *nature*.'

Sunday stared at her in disbelief. 'You're defending him?'

'I'm just saying *Takapa*'s the evil one – taking that nature and trying to turn it into something he can control.' She ran a hand wearily through her auburn hair. 'There will always be 'wolves in the world, Sunday. And there'll always be bad stuff we can't stop, hiding out there in the shadows. We've just got to know what it is we're fighting – and pick the fights we can win.'

Tom clenched his fists. 'This is one fight we *have* to win. I'm going to get Kate back. Whatever it takes.'

'Amen to that, Tom.' Stacy bent back over her microscope. 'You know, these skin cells are reproducing at an incredible rate ...'

'Regenerating themselves?' Tom asked.

'Exactly. But so fast ...' She looked up, rubbed her eyes. 'I *hate* that I can't explain this.'

'Never mind explaining it,' said Chung, pacing around behind her. 'How do we *stop* it?' He noticed a large metal door in the wall behind him. 'Hey, what's this?'

'Cold store,' said Stacy vaguely. 'Don't go in. There'll be a whole heap of viruses kept on ice in there.'

Chung frowned. 'Dangerous shit?'

'Nothing too exotic,' she assured him, turning back to her microscope. 'They're researching diseases in children, I think. Polio, chickenpox, influenza strains, stuff like that.'

'Thought maybe we could hit Takapa with something really toxic,' sighed Chung. 'Instead, what have we got? The flu.'

Tom shrugged. 'Maybe we could spread some germs about this gallery place,' he said wryly. 'Try and make Stubbe sneeze himself to death.'

Stacy glowered at him. 'Gee, the answer was under our noses the whole time.' Then she straightened up from the microscope and frowned. 'Well ... maybe not our *noses* ...' With that, apparently lost in thought, she went into the cold store.

Chung shivered in the blast of chilly air that escaped the metal door, and slipped on the grey sweater Sunday had picked up for him. 'It's a good fit,' he admitted. 'A good choice, too.'

'Yeah, well.' She shrugged. 'They were all out of black leather and wolf's heads.'

'I won't be wearing that stuff again,' he said. 'The Chapter's over.'

'And maybe a new chapter beginning,' Tom muttered.

'Sure. Maybe.' Sunday looked at him doubtfully. 'But in their book or ours?'

CHAPTER FIFTEEN

Kate came round slowly, her head pounding and aching in every muscle.

She supposed that meant she was still alive.

Her eyes flicked open. It made no difference; everything was still black. Distant sounds carried to her – bangs and talk and drills going ... the sounds of things being built, somewhere nearby. Was she still at Brook Mansion, or someplace else?

Weakly, she tried to get up. A crack of light lay balanced on the blackness ahead of her – suggesting a doorway.

Her legs didn't move properly, nor did her arms. For a sick second she thought she'd been paralysed. Then she realised she'd simply been tied up – her feet bound together and her hands tied in front of her.

Hopping and shuffling, fighting a wave of nausea and dizziness, she managed to reach the door. She pulled down on the handle with her two bound hands but – big surprise – it didn't open. She felt with her tender head for the light switch and soon found it. With a whirr, a white strip blinked on above her into blinding light. When her aching eyes had adjusted she saw she was in a storeroom – from the smell of bleach and polish, a cleaner's closet.

She slumped against a wall and sat down, trying to pick at her bonds with her fingertips.

Then she heard a rustling noise coming from a corner of the room.

She froze, suddenly alert, then looked to where the noise had come from. Something moved, half-hidden by a pile of blankets. Then it called feebly for help. It was a man's voice.

Kate shuffled cautiously closer, barely keeping her balance, and saw it was a cute-looking black guy with a classy little beard. Beneath his leather jacket his denim shirt was in tatters, stained and crusty with blood from some pretty deep wounds.

With a shock she recognised him. 'Zac?' she whispered incredulously.

Slowly, his eyes flickered open and looked up at her. 'I've seen you ... before ...' he said haltingly. He was clearly in a lot of pain.

Kate nodded. 'I was there when you visited the Drake Hotel, and when Chung led the attack on Takapa's place,' she told him. 'I saw you attacked, brought down by those 'wolves. I thought you were dead,' she added quietly.

Zac's tongue flicked over his dry lips. 'Man, I hurt bad.'

'You've lost a lot of blood,' Kate said gently. She guessed he couldn't have long. 'I'll try to get some help.' Some hope, she thought. Pulling away from him, she shuffled towards the door. But before she could even reach it, a key turned in the lock. Kate flinched away as the door swung open.

Framed in the doorway against the clean brightness of the gallery beyond stood a skinny man, probably in his fifties, dressed in an expensive black suit that made his deathly pale face seem even whiter. His white-blond hair was shaved down to the scalp, but it had more freedom on his weak chin where it sprouted in a small goatee. His features were small and precise, bunched up close together in the centre of his pock-marked face. Kate shuddered as he stood there, staring at her, his albino eyes sweeping up and down her body. Takapa had come crawling out from under his stone at last. Ready for his big night.

'How charming to see you again, my dear,' he said. 'I'm glad you've woken up. You were asleep for some time.'

Kate glared at him. 'Never mind me,' she snapped. 'What about Zac?' She gestured behind her. 'Are you just going to leave him here to die?'

'Zac? Is that his name?' Takapa tilted his head to one side in mock sympathy. The little silver helix that dangled from his right ear gleamed in the light. 'Such a pity he's not going to pull through. That poor security guard gave his life so that Zac might live again.'

Kate frowned. 'Live *again*?'

'Oh, yes,' smiled Takapa. 'Zac was quite dead this morning, I assure you. He would have stayed dead, too, if he hadn't received a transfusion of energy from Araminta's poor security guard.'

Kate suddenly felt icy cold as she remembered the mulched remains of the security guard, recalled her own disbelieving words to Jicaque, back at the Drake Hotel: *You're saying these codechanters can separate a soul from a living body like a dentist pulls a tooth?* Jicaque had guessed that Takapa would be trying to kick-start Stubbe's soul with psychic energy sucked out of some other poor bastard – and here was proof of his intentions.

Takapa was looking at her expectantly.

'So you and Liebermann are doing the full Frankenstein bit now, huh?' she said quietly.

'Indeed.' Takapa beamed at her like a teacher pleased with a star pupil. 'Although naturally, only the psychic energy from another pureblood lupine will suffice to revive the Great Wolf.'

Kate glanced back over at Zac's prone body in the corner. 'I guess Liebermann has been perfecting his techniques ...' She shuddered to think that something like this had so nearly happened to Sunday. 'Didn't get it quite right this time though, did he?' she spat, staring at Takapa with utter loathing. 'Zac's dying all over again, anyone can see that.'

Takapa shrugged. 'Nevertheless, the experiment was a most useful one: Liebermann had extracted the security guard's psychic energy a few hours prior to putting it into Zac, holding it within a codechanting circuit. During this interval without a host, the energy weakened. Enough remained to bring Zac back to a living state – but not for long. Happily, we now know the importance of placing our extracted pureblood psychic energy immediately into the body of the Great Wolf in order to avoid such ... complications.'

Kate stared at him in disbelief. 'Liebermann kept the guard's ... *soul*, just floating around for hours, waiting for a new body?'

Takapa's pink eyes were gleaming. 'Really, my dear, you mustn't be so sentimental. What I am talking about is merely *energy* – a source of fuel. Your idea of a soul is just romantic hokum.'

'Yeah? Well, my idea of an *asshole* is staring me right in the face,' Kate sneered. 'We don't just run on batteries like machines! We're people, with feelings and memories and dreams ...'

'That is simply clutter,' Takapa told her flatly. 'Liebermann's chanted codes strip all that away.' He took a step towards her. 'I shall proceed with Stubbe's resurrection here at the Bane Gallery tonight, as planned. The sacrifice shall take place before my eminent pureblood audience, and the Master shall rise again. The lupine community shall finally appreciate my worth and offer support to my vision for the future.' Takapa walked towards her, and the fine dark cloth of his suit seemed to swallow the light around him.

'Keep back,' Kate hissed. She took a shuffling step backward, lost her balance and fell down against some boxes.

Takapa tutted and shook his head. His left ear was missing altogether, as if it had been chewed clean off. 'I do apologise for leaving you here with the dying, but I had no time to arrange for a room of your own. When I heard you'd been apprehended at Brook Mansion, I had you driven over at once.' He bowed courteously. 'I simply couldn't wait to see you. Your sharp tongue amuses me no end.' He reached out to touch her. His fingernails were long and filed to points as sharp as his yellow teeth.

Kate closed her eyes and willed herself not to give the evil bastard the satisfaction of making her squirm. She felt his fingers brush against her ankles, then grip the thin cord that held them tied. He snapped it with a quick, slicing motion.

She opened her eyes. Takapa was still crouching

over her, fondling the severed cord between his fingers. His other hand closed around her bound wrists, and heaved her up by them.

He leaned in close. Kate shuddered, and didn't bother to hide it. 'Come, let's take a stroll while we talk of the future,' he said. Then he opened the door and gestured for her to follow him out.

Kate's legs were buzzing with pins and needles, but she refused to let Takapa see her discomfort. With a last glance at the pitiful creature in the corner, she strode out after him.

'Since you're blowing so much cash on your luxury hotel, why hold your big moment at the Bane Gallery?' she asked him haughtily. 'I mean, I can understand you not wanting to keep Stubbe in that dump you call a headquarters, but the conference room at Brook Mansion—'

'Does a king sleep so close to the common herd?' Takapa snapped. 'You think I should simply invite my pureblood guests to peep in at the Master's door?' He shook his head. 'Oh no. This is an *event*, one requiring careful stage management. The build-up, the anticipation ... Imagine the excitement of my audience as they are escorted here to witness the impossible ... Oh, yes, they shall see the Great Wolf – but only when *I* allow it. Here, on *my* terms.'

'And speaking of terms,' she drawled, 'I guess with Araminta in your pocket it's not costing you any extra to hire the place, huh?'

'You underestimate my resources,' said Takapa through gritted teeth.

Was it Kate's imagination, or did he seem just the tiniest bit rattled?

'Besides, I find it agreeable that they should see me as a patron of the arts as well as of science. A Renaissance 'wolf ... with so much to offer to the lupine community.'

An edgy-looking man in a dirty white coat shuffled into view from around the corner. It was Walker. From the spaced look in his bloodshot eyes, he'd finally found his fix. If he recognised Kate he didn't show it. He was too busy shifting uncomfortably under Takapa's glare.

'Not slacking off now, I trust, Dr Walker?' said Takapa softly.

'No, Papa Takapa, I would never do such a thing,' protested Walker. 'I've been checking the new scans.'

'How is our patient?'

'Making a superhuman recovery. Superhuman.' Walker began to babble, with, it seemed to Kate, a mixture of fear and genuine enthusiasm. 'The stem cells have healed whole tracts of the cerebral cortex together with Liebermann's codes. Stubbe's body is healing at an incredible rate. Tissue regeneration is proceeding faster than I first predicted, and—'

'So he'll be ready in time, yes?' snapped Takapa.

Walker flinched like he'd caught his fingers in a mousetrap, and nodded. 'Ahead of schedule, Papa Takapa.'

'Very good. All right, Walker. Carry on.' As the scientist shambled past them, Takapa turned back to Kate with an apologetic air. 'I would show you the body of the Great Wolf himself, but I understand from Araminta you have enjoyed that singular pleasure already.'

'Oh yeah. It was a total thrill.'

Her sarcasm seemed lost on Takapa. 'And in any case, I fear Liebermann might find your presence distracting after this afternoon's encounter. He so hates to be shown up in front of his lesser associates.'

'There was nothing lesser about what they did to my head,' Kate said with a shudder.

'They are talented creatures, no doubt of it,' said Takapa, 'but compared to Liebermann they are ignorant savages. He draws on their powers periodically to boost his abilities in psychic surgery ... and to heighten his strength in preparation for other rituals. As you shall see tonight.'

'Can't wait. But if he's so powerful, how come he's working for you and not the other way around?'

'He was rotting in South America when I tracked him down,' said Takapa. 'Almost dead. I nurtured him back to health, found the last surviving members of his original cult to give him support. He shared my aims in his heyday – to make the 'wolf as powerful and destructive as it can truly be. Now, with my funding and direction, his work can continue. I have restored purpose to that old carcass of his. I have made it possible for him to pass on some of the codechanters' secrets to a new generation, so that his work might never die.'

'Those men, watching Sunday when she was kept at the warehouse,' Kate realised.

He smiled. 'And, thanks to me, Liebermann will achieve tonight his crowning glory – the resurrection of the Great Wolf himself.'

Kate faked a yawn. 'I'm sure it's a big honour.'

'It will be an incredible achievement. But merely the prelude to the real miracles I shall provide for our people.' He grinned at her. 'As our numbers dwindle under human oppression, so I shall boost them through genetic manipulation. As the ambition of most 'wolves fades to simple survival, so I shall create an army of newbloods and control them through the bloodlust drug.'

'I've heard that before,' Kate sneered.

'New York was a trial, an experiment,' said Takapa. 'Jicaque spoiled my supply of the drug with his herbal potions, it is true – but in doing so, he has helped me a great deal. Now I am aware of the drug's deficiencies, I can develop a new strain that no one may tamper with. It will take time, but I *will* have my army, Kate.'

Kate saw the maniacal glow in his unblinking, pink eyes, the determination.

'You're crazy,' she breathed hoarsely.

'You're mistaken.' Takapa gripped hold of her shoulders and pulled her towards him. His meaty breath made her want to hurl. 'Everything I do is to ensure the long-term survival of the werewolf race. Once I have strengthened the genetic makeup of future pureblood generations – putting your wereling friend's DNA to good use – I must ensure they are properly educated. They must have the ambition to fight humanity, to reclaim the world that once was theirs.' He seemed to look past her, as if already surveying some magnificent new werewolf order.

'Purebloods will never accept your tampering with their bloodline,' Kate argued, pulling herself free of his bruising grip. 'Don't you see? It's sacred to them – the history and tradition.'

Takapa smiled. 'And what could be more historic, more steeped in tradition, than the figure of Peter

Stubbe, raised from the ancient dead? When it is understood that the Great Wolf himself understands and appreciates my ambitions, the purebloods will have no grounds for grievances.'

'And they'll open their wallets for you with smiles on their faces, right?' Kate backed away, wringing her tied hands. 'Why are you even bothering to tell me this?' she yelled. 'You couldn't guess what my reaction would be?'

'I tell you because I wish to *share* this with you,' cried Takapa, holding out his hands to her, 'because I have chosen *you* to share my life.'

She laughed in his face. 'If you were the last man or 'wolf on the planet—'

Takapa cuffed her hard on the cheek, stopping her laughter short. 'You have no choice,' he snarled. 'Once I am wed into a pureblood family, the last possible objections to my supreme leadership over the lupine race will fall away.' He cupped her cheeks in his sweaty hands, and his voice grew colder and harder. 'You shall be mine. And you shall bear us so many children, Kate …'

'I'd rather die,' Kate whispered, hot tears stinging in her eyes.

She heard him tutting softly. 'Death, my dear, is a luxury that I shall never allow you.'

CHAPTER SIXTEEN

Tom felt antsy and restless. Chung, exhausted from his ordeal at Brook Mansion and their subsequent escape, had fallen into an uneasy sleep. Sunday was busy helping Stacy with her work, poring over beakers and test tubes. Stacy had been gripped with a sudden school-girl enthusiasm, but she was keeping tight-lipped about whatever the hell she was doing. It seemed she didn't want to raise any hopes, just to send them crashing back down to earth if her idea didn't work out.

So Tom sat uselessly on an uncomfortable stool, haunted by the memory of Kate's arms around him in the penthouse as the 'wolf-change engulfed him.

The idea that he might never see her again when there was still so much left unsaid between them – together with this endless, nervous waiting – was driving him out of his mind. 'I've never felt so useless in my life,' he declared. 'I think I'll go find Blood and Jicaque over at the Bane Gallery.'

Stacy shrugged, a gesture that turned into an awkward stretch. She looked completely beat. 'I hope I'm not going to be too much longer.' She checked her watch. 'Seven o'clock. I *can't* be too much longer.'

Sunday looked at Tom. 'What's the point in your

going? You'll just be waiting around there instead of here.'

'There's a chance Kate could be taken to the gallery,' he said doubtfully, 'and if she is, I might be able to snatch her back. I mean, there's a chance, right?'

Sunday didn't look overly optimistic, but managed a smile. 'Take care. We'll see you soon.' She glanced at Chung. 'You taking him with you?'

'No,' said Stacy, 'he isn't. Chung stays here. I need him.'

Sunday frowned. 'Why?'

'I just do,' mumbled Stacy distractedly, peering again down her microscope.

'Well, since I'm so totally redundant,' Tom said, 'can I take your cell?'

'Sure.' She tapped a slide. 'Got enough cells to be worrying about here in any case.' She passed him the tiny phone. 'I'll call from the landline when we're on our way, but you'd better take the number here just in case.'

Tom did so, and went outside cheerlessly into the neon-coloured night.

Chicago was buzzing in these last few hours before Christmas. The busy streets were slick with rain and humming with restless energy. Tom could see it in the faces of the passers-by – everyone seemed focused and intent, thinking about what was left to do before abandoning themselves to the holiday.

He fell in with the crowd, lonely and adrift, and together they strode past bright shop windows, and bare trees whose skeletal branches were entangled with strings of fairy lights. Cars and buses blared past.

The cold air steamed with the smell of street vendors' hot dogs and roasting chestnuts.

Tom drank in the atmosphere like a man condemned, who might never get another chance. The skyline ranged away, bright and proud. He could see the giant corncobs of Marina City stretching up high over the river, and the sparkling cream façade of the Wrigley Building, bathed in brilliance from a hundred low-level spotlights.

He reached for the cell in his pocket and dialled a familiar number, made strange through disuse.

His mother's voice sounded in his ear, bright and chipper. 'Hello?'

Tom took a deep breath. 'Mom, it's me.'

'Tom.' She sounded twenty years older in a single second. 'Oh God, Tom, where are you, baby? Are you all right? We miss you so much, we're trying to act like everything is OK but it just *isn't*—'

'Mom, I'm OK, I promise,' he said. 'I ... I just wanted to say ...'

He paused. *Goodbye?* How could he do that to her? She sounded so distraught already ...

'Tom? Are you still there?'

'I just didn't know when I'd get the chance to call again, Mom.' He swallowed hard, keeping back the tears. 'And ... well, it's Christmas, right?'

'Come home to us, baby,' croaked his mother down the phone. 'We can sort this whole thing out. The police only want to know your side of the story ...'

'Trust me, Mom, no one is ready for this story. Is ... is Dad OK? Joe?'

'We need you back with us, Tom.'

'Mom ...' He stopped still in the middle of the

street, as the crowds surged past all around him. 'I promise that if ... if I can – if it's within my power – I *will* come back to you.'

'What do you mean, "if I can"? Where *are* you?'

'I love you, Mom. I'm so sorry. Sorry for messing up. Sorry for everything.'

His numb finger stabbed clumsily at the 'end call' button. The phone gave a curt beep and went dead.

Tom pushed it in his pocket, wiped his nose on the sleeve of his hoodie and quickened his step towards the gallery district.

Kate was being herded down a corridor towards an imposing mahogany door. When Takapa opened it, she saw it gave on to a warmly-lit office overlooking the sparkling street below.

A *crowded* office.

Araminta Black glared at her from behind an antique oak desk. Russ Fayn was tied to a chair in the centre of the room, his face streaked with bloody welts and tears. And behind him, hovering grimly like an angel of death, was her mother. Her dad was sitting on a modern, uncomfortable-looking chair in one corner, and started suddenly when she entered.

'I thought perhaps a reunion was in order,' said Takapa. 'It is Christmas, after all.'

'Dad,' Kate blurted, 'Dad, tell me you're not going along with this craziness!'

He looked away, and Marcie laughed. 'Oh dear. Looks like Daddy's little girl can't wind him around her little finger anymore.' She crossed to Kate and seized hold of her hand. 'How many times did I think I'd have to bite that finger clean off ...'

Kate ignored her, nodding instead towards Fayn. 'What's he doing here?'

'Filling in for his egocentric friend, Mr Chung,' said Takapa. 'A pureblood sacrifice.'

'So he's going to end up a pile of mulch and his psychic energy goes into Wolfenstein's monster,' Kate concluded. She looked at Fayn. 'So this is what you sold out your friends for, huh?'

'They said I could head up the Chapter,' whined Fayn. 'That they'd recognise *me* in the new order ...' He slumped back in his chair, shivering like it was ten below.

'The Chungs are a respected family,' observed Marcie. 'The boy's well known to many of the purebloods. His sacrifice would have served to inspire our audience still further.' She sighed. 'A Fayn is a good deal less impressive, especially in this state, but he will have to suffice.'

'I won't do it!' he shouted, straining against the ropes that bound him.

'This morning's experiment has proved that the energy needed to revive Stubbe's sleeping spirit must be transferred swiftly,' Takapa told him. 'Your energy *shall* be taken from you and passed on to the Great Wolf at once. You have no choice.'

'Just like that poor security guard had no choice,' Kate muttered.

'There *is* a choice,' said Hal, rising from his chair. 'You're a disgrace to your name, boy. Duplicitous, cowardly ... not fit to call yourself a pureblood.'

'Go to hell,' muttered Fayn.

Hal rested his hands on Fayn's shoulders. 'And certainly not worthy of laying down your life to bring back the Great Wolf.' He cupped his hands under

Fayn's chin and twisted hard. With a sound like eggshells crushing, Fayn's neck snapped.

'Dad!' Kate yelled. She stared in horror as he released Fayn's bloody head and it lolled forwards.

Takapa stared at him. 'I hope you can explain yourself, Folan.'

'Yes, I think I can,' said Hal. Marcie opened her mouth to speak but he rounded on her. 'Shut up!' he yelled. 'I *will* have my say, woman.'

Marcie actually took a step backwards, stunned into silence.

Kate had never seen such anger in her father's eyes before.

Araminta looked down at her desk as if suddenly absorbed in something else, clearly uneasy at this sudden change in Hal.

'The Fayn boy is not a suitable offering for the Master,' said Hal, his jaw trembling. 'I must insist that … that you take me.'

'Dad, no,' Kate croaked.

For once she and her mom were in agreement. 'Hal, you can't be serious, don't be a—'

'A fool?' Hal challenged her. 'I know that is what you think of me. A lupine fool, content to live in isolation from the world of humans, when I could be dreaming up rebellion as you do, Takapa.'

'You cower in the dark like a child,' hissed Marcie.

Hal ignored her, his gaze fixed on Takapa's raw red eyes. 'You have seduced my wife with your ambitions, excited the bloodlust I had hoped to heal in her. Now you have my daughter as well.'

'Only because you let him, Dad!' Kate gasped, before Takapa pushed her aside.

'I'm sorry, Kate. But I *can* see why Takapa has done all he has. Change is essential if the 'wolf is to survive. Humanity has come to rely on technology and so must the lupine race.' He looked around at each of them in turn. 'Our kind faces a stark choice – a slow, eventual extinction as the lights of humanity's progress ward off the final shadows ... or to fight back. To challenge man.' He squared up to Takapa. 'Personally, I believe it is a fight we can never win. A suicidal flight into madness.'

Takapa sneered at him, then glanced at Marcie. 'How did a woman of such fire come to marry a 'wolf so toothless?'

'Oh, I could show you teeth, Takapa,' hissed Hal.

Do it, Dad, Kate willed him. *Do it for me, for all of us.*

'But I have no right.' Hal took a meek step back. 'Not all 'wolves feel as I do, I know. Many will welcome and embrace strong leadership, a chance to thrive again ... however slim that chance is.'

'We are summoning Stubbe from the dead,' snapped Takapa. 'With such a miracle in our grasp, who dares limit our ambition?'

'It *is* a miracle, I agree,' Hal conceded. 'You will raise a magnificent spectre from our past, and I wish to join with him. To bring about his rebirth.'

Kate stared at him helplessly. 'To die?'

'You dare to call the Fayn boy a coward?' Marcie grabbed hold of Hal, spun him around to face her. 'You weakling. You don't dare to face up to the future so you sacrifice yourself to the past!'

'My family have served the Great Wolf since the beginning,' stormed Hal. 'It was a Folan who rescued

Stubbe's body from his tormentors. A Folan who destroyed the fools who had tortured and killed him.'

Marcie nodded. 'Back then, a Folan had courage to act.'

Hal's body seemed to sag. 'I'm so tired, Marcie,' he said. 'I have tried to embrace the coming changes as you have, but I cannot. I am bound by the old ways. The ancient principles of the 'wolf brotherhood.'

Marcie touched his cheek, almost tenderly. 'Principles evolve, Hal, just like anything else. Just like *we* have to.'

Hal shook his head. 'I have made my choice.'

'Then you are a servile fool. And you are only fit for extinction.' Marcie slowly raked her nails down Hal's face. She tasted his blood on her fingertips and closed her eyes. 'Let him do it, Takapa. The Master will revel in the old stench of his blood.'

'Very well,' said Takapa, his eyes dancing between Kate and Marcie and Hal. 'A willing volunteer? So much the better.'

'No!' Kate threw herself at her mother, grasped her by the throat and squeezed with all her strength, the cord binding her wrists biting into her flesh as savagely as her fingers were digging into her mother's neck.

Marcie stared at her, shocked eyes bulging in her gaunt face.

'When you've given me to that albino freak and turned me 'wolf,' Kate shrieked, 'I swear that I will shred you into tiny pieces.' She felt both Araminta and Takapa trying to pull her off and tightened her grip. 'I'll kill you, hear me? All of you! *All of you!*' Then Araminta smacked her hard in the face and Takapa yanked her clear.

Marcie fell choking to the floor, clutching blindly at Fayn's corpse for support.

Kate struggled furiously against her captors as they bundled her out of the room, still screaming her hate for her mother. Before her tears clouded the scene into broad smears of light and dark, she saw her dad standing alone in the room, shoulders slumped, staring after her. Emotionless.

Defeated.

CHAPTER SEVENTEEN

Tom held himself dead still against the back wall of the Bane Gallery as the guards came into view. To the world at large they could've been just a pair of workmen popping outside for a crafty smoke. But Tom saw the sick spark of yellow that lit their eyes as they peered about. The moon was high in the sky, and Tom felt its brightness like a searchlight. Surely they would see him?

He held his breath, cursing himself for his stupidity in thinking he might stumble on some secret way inside the gallery. Blood had already given the place a stealthy once-over and found no way in, and Tom had failed in just the same way. The door around the back was locked and bolted; you'd need a battering ram to get inside.

But he'd been nervous and restless, the bright moon picking at his nerves as he sat in Blood's car beside the silent Jicaque, hour after hour. It was after nine o'clock now, and Tom had needed to do something. A quick scout around just in case, he'd told Blood. Except, as the hour of resurrection approached, so security had gone through the roof.

Tom knew he would get himself killed if he kept taking risks like this. Chucking his life away wouldn't help Kate ...

But then the guards moved away, not prepared to probe the darkness of the alleyway any further.

Tom muttered a thank you to anyone up in the moonlit sky who might be listening, scaled the fence at the end of the alley, and made his way back around to where Blood had parked further down the street.

Blood's electric window hummed down as Tom approached. 'Well?' he asked.

'No way in. Risked my neck for nothing.'

'I did tell you, you silly little sod,' Blood sighed. 'Get back in.'

Tom gloomily did as he was told.

'Cheer up,' said Blood, jerking his head back at Jicaque. 'Our mystic friend's probably out in the astral plane, walking through the walls and sussing out all the weak points in their security.'

Tom glanced behind him at the old medicine man sprawled on the back seat, his eyes tightly closed, mouth set in a grim line. 'Or he could just be asleep,' he suggested.

'Wonderful, isn't it?' sighed Blood. 'He's deep in meditation – while we should be put on *medication* for thinking we might actually be of use here.'

'Hey, it's Christmas,' Tom reminded him. 'A time for miracles.'

'Bollocks to miracles,' snorted Blood. He tapped his fingers on the steering wheel. 'I wonder if they have werewolves in the Seychelles. You know the old saying – if you can't beat them, piss off to an island paradise and pretend it's not happening.'

'I guess you'd live longer that way,' Tom observed.

'But all that sun-drenched luxury ... what kind of life would it be?' said Blood wryly.

Suddenly Jicaque jerked into life, making them jump. 'The time draws near,' he muttered, his voice hoarse.

'I could've told you that, you old duffer.' Blood passed him a half-empty bottle of water. 'Six hours' meditation and that's the only nugget of wisdom you can come up with?'

'Long ago, the shaman of my people would heal the sick by going into a deep trance. They would then travel to the spirit world in search of a cure.' Jicaque drank from the bottle, then smacked his lips. 'Stubbe's soul festers in the atmosphere around that building like a disease. His presence – the spark of life preserved in the fetid depths of the bog – is reaching out even now. Gloating … anticipating his becoming.'

'So did you find it?' Tom asked. 'The cure, the way to stop him?'

'I know what I must do,' said Jicaque cryptically. 'And I have cleansed myself in readiness.'

'Well, I hope you didn't mark the upholstery,' said Blood.

Tom didn't smile. 'I don't see how we're even going to get in there. The whole place is tight as a drum. There are guards everywhere.'

'We *will* gain access,' said Jicaque simply. Then he opened the car door and eased himself outside. 'Takapa's pureblood guests will be arriving soon. We must be prepared.'

'That's us,' called Blood after him. 'Regular boy scouts.'

But Jicaque was already walking off purposefully down the quiet street.

Blood seemed indignant. 'Is the old bugger skiving off, or something?'

'Who, him? Our very own shaman?' Tom forced a wry smile. 'Just pray he doesn't get mugged on his way back from wherever the hell it is he's going.'

Kate had been thrown back in the cleaner's closet to cool off. Zac's body had been cleared out. She didn't know whether to be sorry or relieved.

That had been some hours ago. Now she was feeling sick with fatigue and worry. Her eyes felt sore with crying, and she had turned off the light in the hope that the darkness might soothe them.

She started when keys jangled and the door was opened. But she recognised the shadow framed in the bright doorway.

It was her father.

Kate swallowed, pushed her hair back from her forehead. 'Dad?'

'I've come to say goodbye,' he told her softly, closing the door behind him.

She heard the click of a switch, then the lights flickered on. His deep, dark eyes were fixed on her.

'Dad, please don't do this,' she begged him.

He hushed her. 'Kate, please. This has been a difficult decision to reach, but having done so ... I am at peace.'

'Well, that's just peachy for you, isn't it,' hissed Kate, twisting away from him as he approached.

'I want to help you,' he said. 'We don't have long, so listen.'

She half-turned her head, feeling sick with nerves at what he might mean. Her body felt freezing cold inside.

'I will not have my daughter branded a common criminal,' Hal said firmly. 'Your mother doesn't know, but I got hold of evidence that can clear both your name and Tom's.'

She turned fully to face him. 'How?'

'You know that Takapa was using a webcam to transmit images of the experiment the surgeon and his assistant attempted to perform on Tom in New Orleans. It kept recording long after things went wrong. The images clearly show your mother was responsible for slaughtering those men.'

'Well, that'll sure convince the world,' Kate scoffed. 'You don't think the police might just raise an eyebrow at footage of Mom slitting some werewolf's throat?'

'You know that lupines hold positions of authority in both the police force and the FBI,' he said calmly. 'I've prepared a letter to an acquaintance of mine who has helped cover for your mother's bloodlust before. Once they receive that, and the evidence, I'm confident you'll be exonerated from blame.'

'So where *is* this evidence?'

'Our house in Seattle. I thought it safest to mail it to myself.'

'Great,' Kate said lightly. 'So what, now you can go kill yourself with a clear conscience? For a cause you don't even believe in?'

'I believe in the old ties,' muttered Hal. 'It is my duty ... my *honour* to serve the Great Wolf as my ancestors did.'

Kate knew there was nothing she could say that would make any difference to him. The silence grew heavy as the two of them regarded each other.

'I had such hopes for my family ...' Hal looked away, shook his head. 'And yet look at you. You helped kill your own brother.'

'He was going to kill Tom,' Kate said dully. 'I struck him, distracted him. The rest was an accident. Tom didn't mean to kill him … he's not a murderer.'

'I've come to believe that,' Hal admitted. 'Wes was always so wild, so much like his mother …'

'Guess we've *all* been big disappointments to you,' she said bitterly.

He shook his head a fraction. Then he took something from his pocket and passed it to her. 'If you can't get out,' he whispered. 'Use this. On yourself if you have to.'

Kate found herself taking a small dagger from her father's hand without question. As she did so, her fingers brushed against his palm. For a moment she was a little girl again, holding his hand, carefree as they walked through some half-remembered sunny place.

Then the darkness came back, and her fingers were curling around the little knife's cold metal hilt. 'I still love you, Dad,' she whispered.

He opened his mouth as if to reply – then just nodded. He turned and walked away without another word, out of the gloom and into the light of the gallery beyond.

As the door clicked behind him, she heard Takapa's hateful voice. 'You are prepared, Folan?'

'I am.'

'Then we must dress you for the occasion. Araminta has the shroud. Go to her in her office.'

'Very well,' said Hal stiffly.

'Oh, and Folan …'

Kate's heart sank to the depths when she heard the grind of a key turning in the lock.

'I think Kate should witness your proud act,' purred Takapa.

'That should be her decision, surely?'

'No, Folan. It is mine. My will is all that matters here.' He gave a throaty chuckle. 'Even the Great Wolf will look to me for guidance.'

Their footsteps moved away, echoed into silence.

Kate flicked off the light, and caressed the dagger blade for comfort in the darkness.

'Here come the purebloods,' Tom announced. 'A real coach party.'

'Hades' scrotum, you're not kidding,' said Blood uneasily, as a luxury coach pulled up outside the Bane Gallery. It disgorged a well-dressed huddle of passengers, wrapped up against the elements. To anyone passing, just a crowd of art lovers on their way to a private viewing.

In brooding silence, Tom and Blood watched the stream of purebloods walk up the stairs and congregate in the large reception hall. Once the last passenger had vanished inside, the coach pulled away.

Tom watched it go. Still there was no word from Stacy, and no sign of Sunday or Chung. He resisted the urge to call Stacy, reasoning that if she had anything to say she'd contact them.

It was now close to eleven. The minutes seemed to pass unbearably slowly, but Tom's heart jolted when he saw how much more time had elapsed.

There was a loud tap on the window beside him. He and Blood turned around in alarm, but it was only Jicaque, his leathery fingers pressed against the fogged-up glass.

Blood pressed a button and the window slid down.

'Jeez, where'd you spring from?' Tom demanded, both relieved and cross. 'I just looked down the street – you were nowhere in sight.'

'Sight is such a simple sense to deceive,' said Jicaque with the ghost of a smile. 'You should not rely on it.'

'Thanks for the tip,' Tom said wryly.

'Where have you been, anyway?' asked Blood.

'A joke store.'

'What, open at this time of night?'

'With some persuasion.'

Tom frowned. 'Terrific. So what are you going to do, make Stubbe die laughing?'

'It is possible,' mused Jicaque. 'After all, what are old jokes to us will be new and potent to Stubbe.'

Tom and Blood swapped horrified looks.

The old medicine man's weathered face creased in a big smile. 'You two cannot *take* a joke, it seems.' He straightened, looked towards the Bane Gallery. 'But perhaps it is just as well. It is fast approaching the time we got serious.'

Kate was literally waiting in the wings; bound and gagged and quite helpless.

The wide, makeshift stage she'd seen on her first visit here had been polished and painted. Tasteful black wooden screens had been placed in front at either side to form the wings, so that key players could enter and exit discreetly. Several more screens were arranged behind it to create a private, backstage area, where an emergency exit to the gallery was serving as a stage door.

The gallery now resembled some trendy modern theatre, complete with empty chairs lined up in rows for the purebloods' imminent arrival. The audience was not to be distracted by backstage goings-on. Everything would be stage-managed impeccably. A slick, polished and impressive piece of live theatre would be presented here tonight.

A piece of history brought to life, in every sense.

Kate struggled to keep calm and unflustered. The gag around her mouth and nose was made of bandages, and she found it increasingly difficult to breathe. She'd managed to hide the dagger up her sleeve. Even now she was subtly scraping it against her bonds while workers came and went under Araminta Black's supervision.

At the rear of the stage, the display case for Stubbe's body had been draped in a rich scarlet covering and placed in a vertical position; presumably so he could be shown standing. Araminta directed a lectern to be moved just a fraction to the left, then turned to the three codechanters, who were all once again dressed in their ceremonial robes. She explained their cues to them and where they needed to stand to maximise the drama of their performance.

Liebermann kept tilting his old, craggy face towards Kate, his bulbous nose twitching as if he could smell what she was up to. She froze as Araminta led the codechanters over, and slid the whole knife carefully back up her sleeve.

Liebermann gripped her face with his rough, wizened fingers and tilted it towards him. 'So it is your father we work with tonight,' he rasped. 'His sacrifice is noble.'

Friedrich nodded. 'A contrast to your own baseness of spirit.'

'It certainly is,' fussed Anton. 'Dear me, yes.'

'Perhaps he is shamed into this action by his daughter,' said Liebermann. 'No?'

Kate glared into the uneven ridges of his milky-white eyes. 'No,' she said fiercely.

'I wish I could tell you he shall not suffer unduly,' said Liebermann, and then he grinned and tapped his strawberry nose like one who is in the know. 'But he shall.'

'We want his sweat, his screaming,' said Araminta softly. 'His death agonies must be evident to all. Think how they shall heighten the drama.'

Kate said nothing, but gripped the little knife all the more tightly. She had an idea or two herself of how the drama might be heightened.

She heard a door open, out of her sight behind the screen. Then her mother's voice sounded, grave and low: 'The champagne reception is winding down. Are you ready?'

Araminta puffed up her scrawny chest. 'Give me one minute.'

'Very well. Then the purebloods enter.'

Kate heard measured footsteps approach. Liebermann released her face and straightened. Everyone looked over her shoulder. She didn't need to crane her neck to know Takapa was here.

'You all know what you must do,' he said quietly.

Araminta spoke for them. 'Yes.'

'And Liebermann ... you are *certain* Stubbe will rise?'

The old man nodded. 'All my life has been leading to this moment. The Great Wolf's body will be infused with Folan's life energies. He *will* be reborn.'

'Then let us begin,' whispered Takapa.

Araminta led the three blind mice to the backstage area, but Takapa remained. He rested his hand on Kate's shoulder, caressing her neck with one flaky fingertip. Gradually the sound of people could be heard, coughs and chair scrapes and low conversation as the room began to fill. A feeling of expectancy grew in the impromptu theatre.

The covering on Stubbe's casket ruffled, though Kate could feel no draught.

Project Resurrection had reached its climax, and it was almost show time.

CHAPTER EIGHTEEN

'Shouldn't we at least be *trying* to get inside?' Tom sighed for at least the third time.

Jicaque shook his head patiently. 'When the 'wolves are concentrating on Takapa's presentation ... that is when we risk entry.'

'Cutting things fine, isn't it?' muttered Blood.

Tom sighed. He was about to get out of the car and stretch his legs when Stacy's cell phone bleeped noisily in his pocket.

'That's a point. We'd better set our phones to vibrate only,' said Blood, fiddling with his own cell. 'Then we can keep in touch if we have to separate.'

Tom nodded. 'Stacy?'

'I won't be much longer,' she cried.

'You can't afford to be,' he said. 'We're ready to go in.'

'This isn't exactly ninth-grade science I'm doing here,' complained Stacy. 'I'm going flat out.'

'We'll let you know if we get inside,' Tom told her.

'You'd better. This plan depends on us getting real close to Stubbe.'

'What exactly *is* your plan, anyway?'

'Jeez, Sunday, get that thing off the heat!' cried Stacy.

Tom thought he could hear something bubbling over.

'Gotta run.' She hung up.

Tom looked up to find Blood and Jicaque both looking at him intently. 'She's on her way. Almost.'

Blood tutted.

They waited in anxious silence for fifteen more minutes.

Then Jicaque seemed to reach a decision. He opened the rear door. 'It is time.'

Blood opened the car door. 'Well, I suppose there's no point delaying the inevitable,' he said.

Tom got out of the car too, and he and Blood joined Jicaque as he walked slowly and deliberately down the street towards the Bane Gallery.

After a few steps, Tom noticed Jicaque was holding something carefully between finger and thumb – a small glass ampoule. 'What's that?' he asked.

'I'm sure Miss Stein would refer to it as ammonium sulphide,' said Jicaque, with the first curlings of a crafty smile on his lips. 'But we would know it better as a stink bomb.'

'So that's our great weapon,' groaned Blood. 'We're doomed.'

'Against such overwhelming odds, a conventional attack will get us nowhere,' said Jicaque, and Tom could see the clarity in the depths of the old man's eyes. 'We must use our wits. If it helps, think of all this as a great jazz number.'

'That *doesn't* help,' Tom said.

'Not in the slightest,' added Blood.

Jicaque shrugged. 'We know the start of the song and its tempo, and we know how it must end. But the path we take to reach there ... that will be the result of inspired improvisation.'

They had reached the steps of the Bane Gallery. Two big guys stood in front of the glass doors.

Without warning, Jicaque boldly marched straight up to them. 'Excuse me, buddy,' he said, slurring his words like a drunk, 'got a light?'

'Get out of here, old man,' snapped one of the guards.

Jicaque swayed forwards, almost knocking into them. Tom saw him drop the stink bomb and grind it beneath his heel. Then the guards shoved him brusquely back down the steps. 'Beat it!'

'And a merry Christmas to you too,' called Jicaque, rejoining Tom and Blood.

'Now what?' asked Blood.

Jicaque smiled. 'Patience.'

The guards started sniffing the air, then gave each other accusing looks.

Tom wrinkled his nose. It was bad enough down the street, so what must it be like on their doorstep?

The two men retreated inside the building, muttering recriminations.

'Now they're out of the way for a minute or two ...' Jicaque pulled something else from his pocket. 'I wonder, Mr Blood, could *you* spare me a light? I noticed you helped yourself to several books of matches from the hotel reception.'

'Nosy parker.' Blood took a book of matches from his pocket, and lit one. The sputtering flame illuminated the object in Jicaque's hand – a firework.

'My thanks,' said Jicaque. Then he lit the firework and tossed it down the alleyway that ran alongside the

Bane Gallery. A whoosh of white sparks illuminated the narrow brick corridor.

'Out of sight,' hissed Jicaque, ushering Tom and Blood out of the mouth of the alleyway and up against the neighbouring building.

Tom realised that now the guards had vanished inside the reception area, their field of vision was limited to the immediate area of the steps. They wouldn't see the fountain of bright white light in the alley. But the guards around the back couldn't miss it.

Sure enough there was a scuffling sound from the alley, then stamping, and the firework went out. Two burly men came cautiously out of the alleyway to see where the firework had come from.

Jicaque jumped out in front of them and blew into a party blower. Like a frog's tongue flicking out to catch a fly, the paper uncurled at speed into the nearest guard's face. He yelped in surprise and jumped back, cannoning into his companion. As both men fell over, Blood ducked after them into the alleyway. Tom heard the sounds of a brief scuffle; then Blood re-emerged, his hair mussed up, wielding a half-brick.

Jicaque looked at him disapprovingly but Blood only shrugged. 'I wasn't about to wait for you to beat them into submission with a whoopee cushion,' he said dryly.

Jicaque turned to Tom. 'The way should be clear now. Get around to that back entrance you tried before.'

Tom frowned. 'How did you know I—?'

'Never mind how I know,' hissed Jicaque.

'And what are *you* going to do?'

Jicaque had taken a firecracker from his pocket.

'Why, Mr Blood and I shall slip inside the front way.'

'Oh yeah?' said Blood doubtfully.

'This firecracker will make a fair-sized bang. While our friends with the sensitive noses leave their post to investigate ...'

'We duck inside.' Blood nodded. 'Clever old sod, aren't you.'

Jicaque pressed a firecracker into Tom's hand. 'You do the same around the back.'

'What if your guards hear and come looking?'

Jicaque just lit the firecracker's fuse. 'You have about ten seconds before it goes off.'

'Don't try this at home, kids,' Tom muttered as he pelted down the alleyway with the fizzing firecracker as fast as he could, into the darkness.

Kate was working at the cords binding her wrists with renewed urgency. She hadn't dared use the knife with Takapa standing so close to her. Now he was out on stage, and events were building to a climax – yet still she wasn't free.

She'd sat through Araminta's big build-up to Takapa's entrance, grinding her teeth to hear him described as a visionary, a leader and a man of science who would bring down the old order and build a new lupine empire in its place. She'd shuddered to hear the rousing applause that greeted his presence on the stage.

When it finally died down, he began to speak. He was shrewd; he did not criticise the purebloods' established way of life, the traditions that shaped their existence. He presented a vision, an ideal: a werewolf utopia on a scale that none before had ever dreamed possible. Prowling the stage, thundering his promises, he made it sound as tantalisingly attainable as the next kill.

And as his oration rang out, Kate imagined all those pureblood eyes straying expectantly to the covered casket that stood behind him, waiting to be unveiled.

Takapa talked of a ten-year plan for controlled population growth, of the rearing and education of 'wolf children not in families and classrooms but in packs.

He spoke of the creation of an inferior class of newbloods, controlled by drugs; hapless humans turned for slavery and sport, who would serve both the pureblood caste and 'traditional' 'wolves.

He outlined the ease with which whole platoons of crack werewolf soldiers could be secretly brought together in key cities across not only America but the whole world, ready for a terrorist show of force when the time was right. All he needed was their support ... and some modest financing.

The purebloods listened raptly, apparently seduced by his passion and his prophecies.

Kate recalled from history class that the Nazi party began life as a handful of louts meeting up in the back room of a beer hall. Within twenty years, the whole world was at war because of them.

'The time has come when we must join together in a single pack,' Takapa argued. 'Through unity, we shall have strength. One day, we shall force humanity to recognise the 'wolf – not as creatures of myth and superstition, but as the superior beings. It is *we* who are top of the food chain, not humankind!' He paused for a burst of wild applause, and opened his arms to his congregation. 'The lupine race will rise up from the shadows of the past to become a thriving force in this planet's future!'

Kate gasped as the dagger blade slipped and sliced into her arm. Gritting her teeth, she ignored the pain and carried on chafing at the cords as hard as her bound wrists would allow.

'And when that time comes to pass, we shall found our own recognised, sovereign state.' Takapa paused impressively. 'But first, we must have a sovereign. I am but a worker, a simple architect of new ideals. I offer our race guidance – not leadership. But I know how important it is to you all that scientific progress never blinds us to the importance of our noble past ...'

Hypocrite, thought Kate, straining against the ropes.

'And so we come to the promised moment,' announced Takapa. After a low round of whispers and murmurings, the atmosphere in the gallery grew reverent and hushed. 'It is not simply my pleasure, but my duty to present to you now a figure truly symbolic of the werewolf rebirth that I promise you. A figure that *I* now raise from the ancient dead, for all our sakes. A figure who ruled over us once ... and who shall again.' His voice grew to an exultant shriek. 'The living incarnation of our people's yearning! The Great Wolf himself – Peter Stubbe!'

He yanked away the crimson covering from the casket.

Kate heard the collective gasp go up from the crowd. She felt the blood drain from her face.

This wasn't the same body she had encountered on her last visit to the Bane Gallery. Dressed in a simple but splendid black robe, the ghastly figure still looked corpselike, but the mummified flesh had grown softer and whiter. The distorted face seemed far more human now, its features rising from the decaying skull, proud, full and sensuous. Seeing the figure in profile she saw that a dark mane of hair had been pulled back from the high forehead in a long ponytail.

Takapa revelled in the sounds of awe and wonder that emanated from his audience. 'This afternoon, you heard Araminta Black describe the condition of the body recovered from the dank waters of the German peat bog in which it lay preserved. Here is that same body now, after the dark magics and advanced sciences that I control have been unleashed upon it. Physical regeneration is taking place even as you watch ... and now, you shall witness the spark of life preserved in this vessel ignite into a flame – at *my* command.'

Kate jumped as footsteps sounded behind her. She tried to hide the dagger back up her bloody sleeve but her fingers were numb with fatigue, she was too slow.

Her heart sank; whoever was coming, they couldn't fail to notice her pitiful efforts. But then, with a cold shiver, she realised that her father headed the approaching group. Wearing a white smock, he walked stiffly across to the stage in silence. Four men, dressed in black like executioners, walked behind. They led out Liebermann, Anton and Friedrich, resplendent in dark, bejewelled ceremonial robes.

Kate watched her dad vanish from view behind the cluster of dark figures here to destroy him, and saw the points of Takapa's teeth show in a smile. Where was Marcie? How was she feeling now?

'For my technicians to bring about the final

resurrection,' announced Takapa, 'an infusion of energy is needed. This can only be provided by the noble sacrifice of a pureblood soul.'

Anton and Friedrich led their acolytes over to the casket, surrounding it in a loose circle, while Liebermann and Hal remained at the front of the broad stage.

Hal cleared his throat. 'I am Hal Folan.' His voice boomed around the gallery. 'I glory in the return of the Master, and lay down my life in his service. I am not afraid to die.'

Kate strained against the gag that stopped her from screaming.

'You have heard how Stubbe will unite our race, how he will lead us on a path to greatness.' Hal cast a sideways glance at Takapa. 'All I ask of you is that when you follow that path, you do so with caution, compassion and respect.'

'We thank you, Folan,' proclaimed Takapa through gritted teeth.

Hal looked down into the crowd. 'To my wife, I say farewell ...'

Marcie's voice carried cold and clear from the hushed audience. 'Goodbye, Hal.'

'And farewell too to my daughter. May her life be better from this day on.' He glanced at Kate and gave her a small, encouraging smile.

Kate's vision of him blurred as her eyes filled with tears, but she could hear Takapa all too clearly as he addressed his audience once more.

'Now, with no further ceremony ... let pure and noble blood soak the flesh of our Master. Let life be wrested from the dark lands of death through this sacrifice. Let the Chant of Resurrection begin!'

Kate worked feverishly at her bonds. Surely they would give way soon. She would break free and run out on the stage, she would sink this knife into Liebermann's back, grab her father and they would run …

That was how it would work if this was a movie. But the bonds held tight, and Kate remained utterly helpless.

Liebermann started speaking his strange, strangulated words, his voice low like it had been recorded and played back at the wrong speed. Slowly, Friedrich took up the chant in a different key, the sounds and syllables carefully discordant. Then Anton added his own voice, an octave higher.

The acolytes began to intone with them, and like a demonic choir their voices rose in volume. Liebermann held a great, curved knife in both hands. The blade inched towards Hal's neck. The point prodded his soft skin. Slowly, excruciatingly, Liebermann scratched an alien, intricate symbol on to Hal's throat.

Kate gave up with the dagger, pulling against the frayed cords like she could break them through brute force alone. Her trembling wrists chafed and burned.

And now it seemed Hal was burning too.

He had started to shake. The chanting grew louder. The symbol on his neck seemed to glow, like a white-hot brand. Hal's mouth had opened but no sound emerged, only smoke, like his insides were on fire. Liebermann's chanting quickened, the words tripping from his old tongue in blade-sharp syllables, two for every one that his acolytes uttered.

Kate strained and strained against the ropes, shouting for her father through the thick fabric of the gag.

A thick spurt of blood erupted from the back of Hal's head like he'd been shot, but before the dark fluid could splatter on the ground it was gone, swallowed up by a radiance emanating from the glass casket. The figure inside was no longer visible, and nor was Hal Folan, engulfed in sparkles of unearthly light. As Liebermann bellowed out the last words of the incantation, Kate watched her father slip away.

The codechanters and their disciples fell abruptly silent, the echo of their words hanging in the air like the smell of death.

The ethereal glow faded from the stage.

Where Hal had stood there was now only a black pile of sludgy, mulch-like debris.

The body in the glass casket twitched. Its skin was soft and pink like a child's.

Dark eyes snapped open.

Peter Stubbe had been reborn.

CHAPTER NINETEEN

Tom tried to stem a feeling of rising panic. He'd let off his firecracker, hidden in the shadows beside the fire exit, and no one had come looking. He had no way of getting inside.

He felt a vibration in his pants pocket, and snatched for the cell phone. But before he could answer it, the sound of running footsteps came piling down the alleyway, heading his way. Tom looked around for some kind of weapon. If it was one of the guards Blood had slugged, with a headache as large as their muscles and out for revenge ...

He clutched the cell phone like it could somehow protect him as a lithe, dark figure rounded the corner.

It was Chung.

'Shit, man,' breathed Tom. 'You scared the hell out me.'

'Sorry about that.' His tattered black leather jacket hung raggedly over his sweater.

'I thought you weren't wearing that stuff anymore?'

'Unfinished business,' said Chung. 'Something I've got to do. Aren't you going to answer your phone?'

Tom hit the green button. 'Yeah?'

'It's Blood. Jicaque's plan worked a treat. Where are you?'

'Outside,' Tom reported. 'No one was interested in my firecracker. But Chung's here.'

'All right. I suppose there can't be any guards at the back exit, or they'd have heard you. I'll try to make my way there.'

'What about Jicaque?'

'He's heading up for the main event.'

'Shouldn't we all stick together?'

'One big fat target, you mean? He didn't think it wise,' said Blood. 'We may well have to be the cavalry, so I hope you're up to it. See you shortly if all goes well.'

The phone went dead. Tom glanced up at Chung. 'Hopefully we'll be getting inside soon.'

'Good,' said Chung. He shivered, dug his hands deep in the pockets of his ripped leather jacket. 'Like I say, there's something I've got to do. For the Chapter.'

Tom looked at him suspiciously. 'What's going on, Chung? Where are Stacy and Sunday?'

'They're coming. I'm just a faster runner than they are.' He smiled grimly. 'Midnight on Christmas Eve. Couldn't get a cab for love nor money.'

'Midnight? Jeez,' Tom said, kicking at the fire door. 'It'll all be starting in there ...'

The door shook suddenly with the jump of a bolt. Tom and Chung backed away.

Blood poked his head out. 'No one about. Now get your stupid arses inside quick.'

Tom looked at Chung. 'Shouldn't you stay here, get Stacy and Sunday inside?'

'I've got things to do,' said Chung, and pushed past him and Blood to get inside the building. 'Where's the action?'

'I don't know. We last saw Stubbe on the first floor, but ...'

'It's as good a place as any to start looking,' said Chung, and he ran off up the stairs.

'Who's your friend?' joked Blood.

Tom heard Chung's echoing footsteps fade. 'That's what I'm wondering.'

Together they took the stairs two at a time. But as they reached the first floor, a figure lurched out from the shadows.

It was Walker. He grabbed hold of Blood's jacket and sank to his knees. 'Help me,' he hissed.

'Oh God, this is all we need,' sighed Blood.

'I've done all they wanted and now ... I'm nothing to them,' said Walker, staring fearfully at Tom and Blood. 'They'll kill me, like they killed the others.'

'Look, the door's not guarded anymore,' whispered Tom. 'Go down there and wait outside, we'll get help for you.'

'No, they'll kill me!' Walker raised his voice. 'Don't you see?'

Blood clamped a hand over the man's mouth, shushing him desperately. 'He's off his head with that drug, fatigue, God knows what else ...'

'Get him outside,' Tom said. 'I'll get after Chung and try to find Kate.'

'What? Leave all the heroic stuff to a little prat like you?' Blood shook his head. 'Come on, Tom, *you* babysit the doctor and let *me* steal into the lion's den. I'm the responsible adult around here.'

Tom smiled. 'You're about the least responsible adult I know.' He turned to leave. 'Take it easy.'

'Tom, wait!'

But Tom was already bounding up the steps, his heart racing. He knew there was no going back now.

'Behold,' said Takapa reverently, 'your new leader, the Great Wolf himself. Peter Stubbe, the founder of our kind.'

Kate stared, transfixed with horror as Araminta removed the glass front of the casket and the man inside slowly stirred. His chest began to rise and fall, awkwardly at first but soon falling into a deep, easy rhythm. The acolytes discreetly cleared the debris Hal had left behind from the front of the stage and took seats at the side, while Liebermann quietly retired to the rear with Anton and Friedrich. All three looked pale and spent.

Takapa kept the patter coming while Araminta gently helped Stubbe out of his transparent coffin. 'A soul that has slept for hundreds of years has arisen in a rejuvenated body. He has come to us to preach the way of the lupine once more. On this day of human celebration, I give you … the Great Wolf.'

Stubbe took two tottering steps towards the front of the stage and stood there, swaying like a drunk. His dark eyes stared at his expectant audience. The atmosphere was electric. Kate felt again that deep, ancestral fear course through her as his presence made itself felt.

But the Great Wolf said nothing at all.

'A brief period of disorientation is to be expected,' said Takapa, smiling confidently.

Stubbe flexed his fingers. He seemed transfixed by the simple movement of clenching and unclenching each fist in turn. A whispered wave of murmured awe swept through the astonished audience.

Then Kate's blood chilled in her veins as Stubbe turned to look across into the wings, straight at her.

His face darkened. '*Mädchen*,' he croaked. '*Meine Tochter* ...'

'He speaks in his native tongue,' proclaimed Takapa, a little uneasily.

'Not so,' chimed in Liebermann, creating a fresh stir in the audience. 'He uses modern German. *Our* native tongue.'

'We have given him knowledge of the situation here,' explained Friedrich, rubbing his skinny old hands together.

'Brought him up to speed, you could say,' agreed Anton.

Liebermann nodded. 'Our magics are as old as he. They link us ...'

'*Tochter* ...' The word seemed to drag itself again from Stubbe's mouth. He reached out a hand towards Kate, pain and confusion in his face.

'It is the girl,' hissed Liebermann, gesturing to Kate. 'He is experiencing some conflict, believing her to be his daughter.'

'Simply the after-echoes of Folan's feelings, lingering in his subconscious,' said Friedrich. 'The effect will pass.'

'You should remove the girl from the wings, Takapa,' said Liebermann. 'Take her from his sight.'

Anton nodded quickly. 'Yes, yes, definitely.'

The audience were beginning to mutter more loudly now. Takapa angrily indicated to Araminta that she should move Kate.

The skinny woman walked off stage with an air of quiet calm, though as soon as she was in the wings, she gave Kate the filthiest look. Then she walked around to grab the back of the chair Kate was tied to.

'My friends,' Takapa implored his audience from the stage, 'soon you shall witness the Great Wolf's inauguration as our one true leader.' He raised his voice. 'Who in this room will not swear loyalty to him?'

More mutters of concern. It didn't take a genius to figure that by doing so, the purebloods would be committing themselves to Takapa's vision as well. He'd given them the sales pitch, and the biggest publicity stunt imaginable. Would they go along with him now?

Araminta tilted Kate's chair back on two legs and heaved her away, out of Stubbe's sight. He was still staring after her. His pained expression stayed with Kate as she was dragged backstage behind the screens.

Then Araminta looked down, and saw the frayed ropes, and the dagger in Kate's raw and bleeding hands. 'You little bitch,' she breathed. 'Thought you could escape, did you?' She snatched the slippery knife away and held it to Kate's throat. 'You need to learn some respect.'

Kate closed her eyes. There was a dull thud and a short gasp of pain.

'And you need to learn to lock your stage door,' said Chung, lowering his fist.

Kate stared first at Araminta's crumpled body, then up at her rescuer. He looked pale and tired through the bruising on his face, but he still made a pretty fine white knight. He yanked the gag down over her chin and she gulped down air. 'Thank God you found me,' she gasped.

'Never mind that,' he said, taking the fallen dagger

and cutting roughly through her ropes. 'Is Stubbe out there?'

She shuddered, nodded her head.

Chung studied the small dagger. 'I could use this on him ... but the codechanters would heal him in a moment.'

'And you'd be dead just as fast,' Kate pointed out.

He handed her back the dagger. 'So I guess I'm sticking to Plan A.'

'You're seriously going out there?'

Chung's answer was to march out of the wings and on to the stage. Gingerly rubbing some feeling into her bloody wrists, Kate crept forwards to see.

'Great Wolf!' Chung cried, pressing a chaste kiss against the startled man's hand before sinking to his knees. 'My master, my saviour!'

From her vantage point, peering around from behind one of the screens, Kate could see the audience now. They were a mixed crowd, all adults and dressed smartly like they'd come out to the theatre. And they were sure being treated to a show.

But Kate's eyes were on her mother in the front row, on the way her gaunt face was streaked with tears. For a second Kate wished she could reach out to her, share the pain she felt at Hal's passing. But Marcie's face was already twisting with rage. She was looking at Takapa expectantly, but he shook his head a fraction. Kate guessed he didn't want things to get messy at this crucial point.

'Perhaps some of you know me,' Chung yelled on his knees, his voice hoarse. 'I am Ryan Chung, a pure-blood as you are. I recognise the Great Wolf as my absolute master.'

The audience were nodding and whispering, clearly impressed. Stubbe just stared at his worshipper, bewildered, but Kate saw something small in Chung's hand catch the light.

'You see,' Takapa shouted. 'The worthy Ryan Chung, proud torch-bearer for the 'wolves of this city, is here to pay homage.'

Chung smiled. 'And I trust every pureblood here will follow my example.'

Stubbe gave a sudden bark of pain and surprise. Chung moved his hand away from his master's ankle, and Kate saw he'd stuck the fastening pin of his silver wolf's head brooch into the soft pink skin.

Takapa lashed out with his foot, kicked Chung under the chin and sent him sprawling off the stage. Many in the audience cried out or jumped up in shock. As Chung fell heavily to the floor, Marcie pounced on him.

'*Nein*,' thundered Stubbe.

The room fell silent.

Marcie scuttled meekly back to her seat.

Takapa stood staring down at Chung's unconscious body, seething with rage but suddenly impotent.

Kate, too, could only watch helplessly. She was free now, but just as powerless. Her mind raced; there had to be *something* she could do ...

Stubbe stooped to pluck the brooch from his ankle, pressed his finger to the bead of blood that had welled there. Slowly he rose and smeared the blood over his tongue. '*Blut* ...' He shuddered, his dark eyes wide and gleaming as he seemed to take in his surroundings properly for the first time.

When he spoke again it was in halting, heavily

accented English. 'This is … a place of devilment. There is light … without fire. Your garments … are alien to me. A stink, unnatural … is on the air.'

Kate shivered. Was English something else the codechanters had passed on to Stubbe? Or had the understanding been taken from her father?

Now Stubbe looked at Takapa. His grasp of the language seemed to be improving. 'You … brought me here?'

'You owe your rebirth to me,' proclaimed Takapa vaingloriously. 'Hundreds of years have passed since you were taken from us. Now your presence is restored, our plans can—'

'Your plans?' Stubbe snorted scornfully. The grief Kate had seen in his face had hardened, and he stood imperial, regal. She knew without a doubt that the true Stubbe was now before them, the indomitable Great Wolf of legend. 'Your plans smell as bad as the air, little man,' he went on. 'Just as there is no meat on your bones, there is no bite in your prophecy.'

Takapa gave a little strangled gasp as excited whispers and mutterings again rose from the audience. He glared at Liebermann. 'I am confident that when *I* have made clear to you my ambition—'

'I care more for the boy's ire and action than for your words, whey-face.' Stubbe licked his finger again and smiled down at Chung's unmoving body. 'You fawn like a child and show me only smiles. The boy has shown me … even here in your bad-tasting world … that blood is still blood.'

'Yes!' Takapa seized on the phrase, turned and addressed the audience once more. 'You have all heard the Great Wolf speak. Blood is still blood, and we shall make oaths in it. We shall proceed as planned with the crowning ceremony.'

'Wait!' Someone else had entered the gallery. The deep, commanding voice echoed through the room. Even Stubbe looked perturbed.

Takapa's face had turned close to the colour of his eyes at this latest disruption to his plans. 'Jicaque?' he hissed in disbelief.

'Oh, sweet Jesus,' Kate breathed.

Then she felt a hand come down hard on her shoulder.

Tom stood just outside the main gallery, pressed up against the wall out of sight, cursing that he hadn't gotten here just a few moments earlier. Jicaque had gone inside, alone – and now Tom didn't have the first idea of what he could do.

'Yes, my name is Jicaque,' he heard the old Native American announce, to fresh hubbub from the pure-blood mob. 'Some of you may know my name, and that I am descended from the Shipapi – the people who long ago sought to destroy the man who stands before you now.'

Tom closed his eyes. Nice going, Jicaque. Gatecrash someone else's party, then switch off the music and turn all the lights on. How to make yourself real popular.

He crouched down and peered around the side of the door – then swallowed hard as he saw the place was packed with people who would gladly kill him the moment he stepped inside.

There had to be fifty people seated or standing in the gallery, their attention divided between Jicaque – a scruffy, diminutive figure in the middle of the gang-way – and some dark-haired guy in a black gown. It could only be Stubbe. Chung's body lay spread-eagled on the floor, but at this distance, Tom couldn't tell if he was dead or just sleeping. The codechanters and Takapa stood watching intently from the stage. Marcie stood before the stage, angling for a better view.

Tom saw Takapa gesture to two heavy-set men in the front row and heard him hiss, 'Seize the old fool. Get him out of here.'

'No!' boomed Stubbe. He held up a hand to Takapa, clearly warning him to stay out of this fight. 'I shall hear his words.'

'You are a man out of time, Stubbe,' pronounced Jicaque. 'I come here now to finish the Shipapi's task.'

'You pit your strength against mine, old man?' Stubbe smiled, showing a set of crooked teeth.

'Next to you, I am a stripling in the full flush of youth,' countered Jicaque.

'I remember ... when they came for me,' said Stubbe, walking to the edge of the stage. 'Yes ... I was tortured ... my legs and arms beaten till they broke, as they sought to cripple the 'wolf inside me. I saw ... *your* face ... watching on.'

'You saw the face of my ancestor,' said Jicaque gravely. 'It was his mistake not to extinguish your evil will for ever.'

'Evil?' Stubbe shook his head. '*Noble*. The heritage of man is false and flat. The bloodline of the 'wolf is vibrant and strong.'

'As it shall be again,' added Takapa.

Jicaque ignored him and turned on Stubbe. 'Was it

noble to feast on children in their beds? To hunt and kill many under each full moon, or else to bite any drunk or harlot passing and so spread your curse?' He shook his head. 'You were never satisfied with the balance of man and wolf. Like this one' – he pointed accusingly at Takapa – 'you wished the lupine to *usurp* man.'

With sudden, surprising agility, Stubbe jumped down from the stage into the gangway. 'And ... should I *not* wish such a thing?'

There were a few ugly murmurs of support from the purebloods.

'It seems we have some entertainment. Watch, my friends,' said Takapa quickly, as if hoping to somehow convince his audience that he was still holding sway. 'I trust you will find amusement in what follows.'

Tom bunched his fists, knew he had to help Jicaque. But how? Jicaque had turned his back on Stubbe now; he was facing the exit, facing *Tom*. But the old man's eyes were closed, even while those of his enemies were fixed on him all around, willing his destruction.

Then Tom saw Jicaque's lips were moving. He was mumbling something under his breath – a spell, a good luck charm?

It had better work fast, he thought.

'Hear me!' boomed Stubbe, glancing back at the codechanters on stage. He licked his lips, slowly and lasciviously. 'My old appetite is keen. I shall taste meat in this bedevilled world – sate my hunger with the blood and flesh of this man. As his ancestor watched me die ... so all of you here shall witness me slay him in turn.' He glared around warningly at his audience. 'Let neither tooth nor claw, nor modern magics distract me from my kill.'

Tom watched in horror as Stubbe's form began to buckle and fold. The air was filled with a sudden reek of decay, and a great, dreadful hush fell upon all those present as his soft pink limbs twisted and tightened. Stubbe's robes tore open along the razor-sharp length of his spine. White, lustrous fur quickly covered his body. Tom remembered the white wolves, magnificent creatures mauled to give this monster life. This Great Wolf was huge, by far the largest lupine he'd ever seen.

'Magnificent!' cried Marcie, sounding deeply moved. 'Yes, the Great Wolf must sate his appetite – and have his revenge!'

Jicaque still had his eyes closed, like a child who thinks if he can't see the monster in the dark, the monster can't see him. But this monster was coming to eat him. Tom could only watch helplessly as the great 'wolf drew closer and closer, with black saucer-eyes and jaws like a 'gator's. After laying dormant for almost four hundred years, Peter Stubbe was again showing the world his true, hideous form.

'Now, how did that story about David and Goliath go?' Tom muttered shakily.

He dug his nails hard into his palms. Bit down on his lip and scissored his teeth through the soft skin. Felt the delicious iron tang of hot blood in his mouth. Shut his eyes tight, willed his already racing heart to beat faster, *faster* … to beat so loud it would wake the 'wolf beneath his skin.

Bringing on the change for what he sensed would be the last time.

CHAPTER TWENTY

Kate spun around and raised her fists, ready to strike out at her assailant.

But it was Blood. She struck him anyway, but lightly on the chest before giving him a brief hug. 'Like I wasn't frightened enough.'

'Sorry if I seemed heavy-handed,' said Blood, worriedly pulling her away from her hiding place and further back stage. 'I tripped over Araminta.' He indicated the skinny woman, still unconscious on the floor. 'Your work?'

She shook her head. 'It was Chung. Then he stabbed Stubbe's foot with his brooch and got kicked off the stage.'

'Strain must've got too much for him,' Blood reflected. 'Still, one bad guy mildly injured, only about sixty to polish off, right?'

'I think we're about to lose one of the good guys,' Kate hissed. 'Jicaque's out there, taking on Stubbe. Where's Tom?'

'He went on ahead. I wound up being weighed down with Walker. He's raving like a madman, but he did tell me about this back way on to the stage.'

'Chung managed to find his way back here all by himself,' Kate muttered. 'I only wish Tom had. Where's Walker now?'

'I clonked him on the head. I'm getting quite good at it.' Kate gave him an accusing look and he shrugged. 'He was a liability. At least he's safely out of it.'

They heard a sudden, chilling roar from the gallery.

'Good gods, I wish *we* were,' muttered Blood. 'Sounds like the mother of all 'wolves.'

'Or the father,' Kate realised. 'It's Stubbe. Jicaque won't stand a chance ...' She looked at Blood. 'Do you have a match?'

'This is no time for a last cigarette,' he chided, producing a matchbook.

'We need a distraction, a smokescreen,' Kate said, ignoring his puzzled look. 'And there's no smoke without fire.'

As Tom bounded into the gallery, the sound of Stubbe's terrifying roar rang in his ears. He crouched protectively in front of Jicaque, bared his teeth and roared defiance at the Great Wolf that towered over him.

Stubbe stared down curiously, saliva dripping from his jaws.

Tom dimly heard Marcie scream that the intruder should be stopped and killed, and a confused outbreak of babbling voices close by. But through it all his sensitive ears focused on Jicaque's incantation, a rhythmic, soothing muttering in some strange language. Though Tom didn't understand the story those words described, he knew it needed to have an ending. He would gain Jicaque time the only way he knew how.

With a bellowing roar he leaped for the tree-trunk thickness of Stubbe's throat.

*   *   *

Backstage, Kate and Blood had set light to the crimson throw that had covered Stubbe's casket, and were frantically fanning the flames. Oily smoke was rising up from it, drifting over the screens towards the high ceiling. The flames were licking against the chair she'd been strapped to.

'We need more stuff to burn,' Kate realised.

Blood pulled off Araminta's jacket. 'If this catches we'll chuck the rest of her on,' he whispered.

Kate wasn't entirely convinced he was joking. 'That cleaning cupboard I was locked up in – might be something flammable in there. Come on, quick.'

But as they shot out through the emergency exit and turned into the corridor, they ran into two people coming the other way.

'Stacy! Sunday!' Kate gasped.

There was a brief frenzy of hugs.

'Jesus,' said Blood, 'can any old Tom, Dick or Harriet wander in here?'

Stacy tugged at her V-neck top suggestively. 'Come on – two drunken party girls out late on Christmas Eve, looking for someone to kiss under the mistletoe? Those stinky guards never stood a chance.'

Sunday nodded enthusiastically. 'Closed their eyes for a kiss, got a chloroformed pad over their noses.'

Blood looked at Stacy approvingly. 'You've been busy.'

'You don't know the half of it,' said Stacy. 'Did Chung get in here OK? He ran off ahead of us ...'

Kate nodded, jerked a thumb back at the fire door. 'He got in through there and went stage diving.'

'Did he prick Stubbe with the pin?' asked Stacy eagerly.

Kate frowned. 'How did you know?'

Sunday looked at Stacy. 'Fingers crossed then.'

'It has to work,' muttered Stacy.

Kate looked questioningly at Stacy, but decided against asking more. 'Stubbe's turned 'wolf,' she said.

Stacy beamed. 'But that's great news!'

Kate stared at her. 'Not when Jicaque's out there facing up to him!'

Sunday looked over Kate's shoulder at where smoke was seeping out from under the door. 'Uh, is something on fire in there?'

'We're looking for something to keep it stoked,' said Blood.

Kate nodded. 'We need anything flammable, guys. You try this way, we'll go down here.'

Another mighty roar sounded from the gallery. Then a quieter, yet somehow angrier one rose in response.

'Shit,' Kate breathed. 'That's Tom. He's in there too.'

Tom twisted clear as one of the Great Wolf's heavy paws rushed down to crush his ribs, smashing instead into a row of seats and sending purebloods screaming and tumbling. He struggled up. This was the third time he'd attacked Stubbe, only to be swatted away like an insect. His body was battered and bruised, and blood was spilling from claw marks in his back, but he couldn't give up.

He *had* to keep Stubbe away from Jicaque.

The old man still just stood there, hunched up and defenceless as he chanted on. But the purebloods' hungry stares were falling on his frail body, and Tom sensed that many of them were ready to change – the excitement, the ferocity of the struggle before them ... Stubbe might've wanted to keep this fight for himself, but now blood had been spilled, how could a crowd like this help themselves?

Suddenly he caught Marcie's cold funereal scent. From the corner of his eye he saw her creeping towards him, a green-gold gleam spiralling through her narrowed eyes as she readied herself to will on her lupine form.

But then a surge of panic seemed to go through the crowd around him. The codechanters were speaking, all three as one, Liebermann leading them in a booming, guttural concerto.

Stubbe took full advantage of the distraction, lunging for Tom's throat, jaws wide and gaping. Tom barely dodged in time, colliding with a couple who fell stiffly like mannequins. Like they were unable to move. He glanced around, and saw that every pure-blood in the place seemed rooted to the spot.

'What are you doing?' he heard Marcie shout, frozen in her crouching position. 'You old fools, release us!'

'The Great Wolf hunts!' shouted Liebermann, briefly breaking from the chant. 'And he commanded that no one intrude. So be still, Folan!'

Tom skittered back towards the stage, barking and growling at Stubbe, trying to lead him away from Jicaque. He knocked against Marcie, who bellowed with impotent anger as she toppled forwards on her face. Then the shout died away, and with it the anguished screams of everyone else in the room. Tom supposed that the sound of fifty people screaming for help would hurt the codechanters' ears. Better to silence them right away with a few chanted words.

'Release the purebloods, Liebermann!' stormed Takapa. 'They are our allies.'

'And the Great Wolf is our *Master*,' said Liebermann reverently. 'You heard the orders he gave.'

'*I* command here!' shouted Takapa desperately. '*I* brought Stubbe back from the dead!'

'No.' Liebermann shook his head and smiled. '*We* did.'

Then Tom heard Liebermann lead his brothers in the chant of the code once more.

'Let me go!' screamed Takapa. 'Release me at once! I reclaimed you from the wilderness. I—'

His voice choked off. Tom spun around to find Takapa, too, was powerless and frozen as stiff as a statue. Tom leaped up on to the stage in front of him.

Stubbe bellowed, reared up and swiped at Tom with his deadly claws.

Mustering all his strength, Tom leaped clear at the last moment. He heard Takapa shriek.

Then the shriek stopped. There was a thud as something heavy hit the stage and rolled off and on to the floor.

Tom turned. Stubbe's claws were bright with blood.

Takapa's pink eyes stared out from his severed head, fixed on Tom in hatred.

Before Tom could even react, Stubbe was charging for him again, filling his ears with a deafening roar. The purebloods looked on helplessly in panicked silence.

Tom skittered aside, dodged nimbly past the Great Wolf. But he was tiring. His body ached and throbbed. He couldn't keep this up for much longer. The acrid smell of smoke caught in his nostrils. There was no time to work out where it was coming from. Stubbe was coming for him again.

And then he saw Kate and Blood running out from the wings and on to the blood-soaked stage.

The fire was taking too long to get going, even with the extra rags they'd taken from the cleaner's closet. It wasn't about to distract anyone, and Tom was in trouble. So Kate and Blood had come running out here to try Plan B; or as Blood put it, Plan God-knows-what-that-might-B.

But they both skidded to a halt in shock at the sight of the giant, misshapen 'wolf tearing through the silent gallery.

'It's Godzilla's hairy cousin,' said Blood faintly.

Through the smoke, Kate took in the horror of the scene in snatches. She saw Tom, his dark skin lacerated and bloody, darting away from the monster like a frightened cub, but hemmed in by the crowds cringing in silent horror. She saw Takapa's headless body standing to attention, his smart suit soaked in blood; Jicaque, seemingly heedless of the carnage around him; her mother, paralysed on the floor, lips unmoving but eyes wide and frightened ...

Kate tore her eyes away, turned to Blood. 'Tom's trying to buy Jicaque time, but with all the people in here, he's got no room to manoeuvre!'

'Ach, the tiresome Folan girl again.' Liebermann came shuffling out of the smoke, leering at her. 'I think now we must stop you for good.'

'Hear, hear to that,' said Anton, stifling a cough.

'Uh-uh.' Blood kicked Liebermann in the crotch and shoved him back into Anton, who toppled and fell. 'I think you've hurt the people I care about quite enough already.'

'He's stronger than he looks!' Kate shouted. 'Watch out!'

Even as she spoke, Liebermann lashed out with his fist with the same frightening force that had crushed Mike's throat. But Blood dived aside – just as Friedrich shuffled forward to come to the aid of his master.

Liebermann's fist was flying too fast to stop. The blow pulverised his acolyte's chin, sent Friedrich flying back into one of the screens at the rear of the stage.

Slowly it toppled over backwards and crashed into the fire Kate and Blood had started. And Friedrich's limp body, swamped by his dark robes, slid into the flames.

'No!' shouted Liebermann. He lunged towards the fire but Kate kicked his feet out from under him and he fell.

Anton, flat on his back on the stage, started to chant at her, the same harsh sounds and syllables he'd used in the penthouse earlier that day. But as the smoke grew thicker, he choked on the words, couldn't get them out, couldn't seem to draw breath.

Liebermann was coughing too, trying to scrabble back up and reach his friend on the fire.

Kate knelt down on the small of his back to stop him from rising. 'Help me, Blood!' she shouted, her eyes starting to stream.

He knelt on one of Liebermann's arms and held down the other with both hands.

'Release me!' Liebermann rasped. 'I must see to Friedrich!'

'As soon as you release the people in this room,' Kate hissed in his ear. She coughed painfully, held the dagger to his throat. 'And don't even think about turning 'wolf. I'll slit your throat before you've sprouted your first hair.'

Liebermann nodded. He started to shout out the sinister words between hacking coughs, the strangulated sounds ringing out through the smoky room. He looked to Anton as if hoping for help; but Anton now seemed just a tubby old man, flat on his back and struggling feebly for breath.

Gradually, like marionettes twitching on unseen strings, the purebloods in the audience came back to life at the sound of the code. They stared around, bewildered and frightened, their movements slow and awkward as feeling returned.

Liebermann's booming voice dried as the smoke got thicker. But he'd done enough.

'Get out of here!' Kate yelled at the purebloods. 'Go on, now, while you've got the chance!'

They didn't need much encouragement from her. The ones least affected were already making for the doors. Kate took the knife away from Liebermann's neck and immediately he slithered across the stage to reach Friedrich. But the old acolyte's brittle body was now consumed in the flames.

Liebermann reached in, determined to haul him out. 'I do not feel the flames,' he boasted, gripping hold of Friedrich's burning body. 'I can block pain. I can—'

But he stopped his bragging as the sleeves of his fine

old robes quickly caught fire. He tried to beat out the flames, but stumbled and fell on to Friedrich's blazing corpse. Liebermann screamed as the flames spread to consume him too. Anton did not react. His chest had stopped moving, his eyes were closed.

Kate tore her eyes away from the horrific scene and looked back at Blood. 'At least Tom's got room to move now.'

'Too late,' said Blood.

Tom had backed into a corner and now he was trapped there. Stubbe was bearing down on him with one massive, bloodied paw raised, ready to strike.

Tom stared up, exhausted but defiant as the Great Wolf towered over him. He had done all he could. But now it was finally over.

Then, as Stubbe's scarlet paw swung down to smear Tom over the floor, a dreadful clanging alarm rang out. Stubbe roared in anger, staring around wildly, fear in his huge dark eyes.

With a thrill of hope, Tom realised Stubbe would never have heard a fire alarm before.

He saw Stacy and Sunday standing by the alarm button the other side of the smoky hall, gesturing frantically that he should get out of there while he had the chance. He took that chance, and bolted past his bewildered foe.

As he did so, he took in the crowds of purebloods making sluggishly for the exit, some on foot, some stumbling on all fours, in sleek lupine form. Marcie's face was screwed up in concentration as she walked. Suddenly Tom saw her eyes glow green-gold, her features warp and shift. She bared her teeth as she freed the 'wolf inside her.

She was making straight for Jicaque.

Kate grabbed hold of Blood's arm in excitement as the fire alarm clanged on. 'Look!' she yelled in his ear. 'Stacy and Sunday must've doubled back around and set it off. Tom got away in the distraction. Way to go, girls!'

But Blood wasn't listening. 'Jicaque!' he bellowed. 'Tom, quick!'

Kate saw why he was shouting, saw the 'wolf racing for the old shaman, and her blood ran cold. 'Mom,' she whispered.

Tom quickened his pace, pushed his 'wolf body to the limit, his fear and loathing of Marcie lending him brute animal strength.

He threw himself through the air, broadsided her, his teeth sinking deep into her neck. She squirmed and struggled but he held on. Her blood was bitter in his mouth, like bile. Her flesh was tough and sinewy.

Rip at her flesh, a part of him screamed deep inside. *Kill her, for all she's done to you. For all she wants to do to Kate. End this.*

He felt her windpipe crushing in his jaws. But then through the screaming, through a blood-red haze, he heard Kate's voice. Something she'd said to him months ago now.

'Your 'wolf is not a cold-blooded killer – because Tom Anderson is not a cold-blooded killer.'

He was better than the 'wolf.

Tom opened his jaws, released her and backed away.

Snarling, Marcie turned to face him, her jaws

234

streaming thick bloody drool, eyes crazed with pain and rage. She tried weakly to scramble up, to continue the fight.

But now she was in the path of a stampede of 'wolves. In their fear, their bodies sluggish and unresponsive, they made no attempt to avoid her. Heavy heels and paws stamped on her hide and her head as they stumbled and staggered for the exit, for escape. Tom crouched in front of Jicaque protectively, barking and snapping at anyone who strayed too near him.

When the panicked crowd had passed, Marcie's bloodied head was twisted at an unnatural angle. She didn't get back up.

The shrill clamour of the fire bell abruptly cut short. Tom saw Stubbe had knocked the alarm from the wall. He roared again, but weaker now …

An eerie calm settled over the near-empty hall. Jicaque had stopped chanting. He opened his deep amber eyes, reached out his hand and placed it against Tom's flank. 'My thanks,' he whispered. 'Your 'wolf is no longer needed.'

Stubbe's bestial body seemed to shrink and snap in on itself. He shook and staggered as his human self pulled itself out from the body of the 'wolf.

And Tom could see there was something wrong. Stubbe's skin was blemished with red bumps. His forehead was beaded with sweat, and his hair hung wet and lifeless around his swollen neck.

Uncertainly, Stubbe advanced on Tom and Jicaque. 'I … do not need the claws of the beast … to finish you.'

'I'll tell you what you need. You need a doctor, man.' Tom whirled around to find Chung was walking

235

towards them. 'Score settled,' he said, as he pulled off his leather jacket and threw it to the floor. 'The Chapter's over.'

Behind him, Tom saw Kate and Blood were clambering down from the stage.

Then Stacy walked in through the main doors. Sunday ran to stand beside her. 'Stay away from him,' she warned Jicaque. 'Don't let him touch you.'

Tom wasn't sure Stubbe was going to make it across the room to touch any of them. The man looked really sick.

Stubbe paused, staring at them, his expression shifting between rage and despair, lesions clinging like red leeches to his face. Then he spun to face the stage. '*Hilfe!*' he shouted, his voice cracking, trying to discern the codechanters through the thick pall of smoke.

No one answered his call for help.

As Tom stared in disbelief, Stubbe sank to his knees, his breath rasping and ragged.

Kate saw Blood run ahead to crouch beside Marcie's body, human again, pale and naked and face down in a sticky pool of blood.

He looked up at her, and shook his head. 'I think she's a goner,' he said. 'Neck's broken.'

Kate didn't want to get any closer. She turned away, walked shakily over to her friends. Inside, she felt numb.

Stubbe clutched his sides as she drew closer. She saw he was weeping.

'*Tochter?*'

Kate stared at him coldly.

'Over now.' He feebly gestured to where Marcie lay motionless on the floor. 'Finished.'

She looked deep into his watery eyes. The light in them was fading. A word formed in her throat but she was almost afraid to say it.

'Dad?'

Stubbe stared at her for some time, his eyes expressionless, like dark holes poked in his florid face. 'Kate,' he whispered.

Then he fell forward and was still.

Kate stared at him, tears welling up in her eyes, and took a step closer.

'No, Kate,' Stacy warned her. 'You don't want to catch what he's got.'

'What the hell happened?' asked Tom. He was human again, wrapping Stacy's scarf around his waist like a sarong. 'Jicaque, did you do this?'

He shook his head, staring thoughtfully down at the body before them.

'It was me,' said Stacy. 'And you, I guess, Tom. That joke you made at the lab about giving Stubbe the flu so he could sneeze himself to death? I got to thinking ... Stubbe lived four hundred years ago, right? Long time before any kinds of inoculation. So I started mixing up those cold-store viruses into a cocktail ...'

'Kind of an *ultra*virus,' chimed Sunday.

'Of course,' Tom murmured. 'His body would have no defence against modern diseases.'

'But how did it work so fast?' asked Blood.

'The rate his cells were reproducing themselves in that skin sample ...' Stacy whistled. 'I took a chance that the same thing would happen once his whole body woke up – all those regenerated cells buzzing away inside him ...'

'So that's why Chung stuck the pin in him,' Kate said dully.

Chung nodded. 'Stacy said I had to get the ultra-virus into his bloodstream.'

She looked for the mark on Stubbe's ankle, but it was lost in a mass of crimson lesions.

'His metamorphosis into the 'wolf worked *for* us,' said Stacy quietly.

Tom half-laughed. 'Not from where I was standing.'

Stacy shook her head. 'The 'wolf metabolism works faster and harder, remember? The virus was able to replicate itself through his body far more quickly.'

'Then if Stacy's ultravirus was wearing Stubbe down, killing him from inside ...' Blood looked hard at Jicaque. 'What were you doing all that time? Counting sheep?'

Jicaque's leathery face crinkled in a smile. 'I told you how in the Old Time the shaman of my people would heal the sick by going into a deep trance and travelling to the spirit world in search of a cure.'

'You were trying to heal Stubbe?' asked Tom disbelievingly.

'Stubbe was not my patient. I was reaching out to the man who gave him life.'

Sunday frowned. 'Liebermann?'

'No,' Kate said. 'My father.'

'I sought to overcome Stubbe from within just as Stacy did,' said Jicaque, 'but by calling on the last and best of Hal Folan.'

'And he heard you,' Kate breathed.

Jicaque smiled sadly. 'Your father was a strong and noble man. Even with all the magics at Liebermann's command, his soul could not be stripped clean from the energies that sustained him in life.'

Kate looked down. 'Always was a stubborn son of a bitch,' she whispered.

'Maybe that's how I kept ahead of Stubbe, Kate, even when I was exhausted,' Tom murmured. 'Your dad was there in him, holding him back, slowing him down.'

She nodded, wiping her tears. 'Maybe.'

'Hey,' said Sunday, peering through the smoke across to the stage. 'What about the fire?'

'Seems to have gone out,' said Chung uneasily.

They heard movement up on the stage.

Araminta emerged, clutching a fire-extinguisher that was almost as big as she was. 'They're dead,' she shouted, choking on smoke. 'Liebermann and the others ... burned or smothered, I can't tell. And Takapa ...' She looked shattered, gazing around at the devastation, the bodies and blood in her once immaculate gallery. 'All our dreams ... our plans ...' She flung the extinguisher to the floor and screamed at them: 'What am I supposed to do now?'

'It's your gallery,' said Blood mildly. 'You can sodding well clean it up by yourself.'

Araminta stared at him, speechless, her bulging eyes ready to pop out of her head.

'We're letting that bitch off the hook?' asked Chung in disbelief.

'You want the cops to find all this?' Blood shot back at him.

Stacy gave Araminta a little wave. 'Merry Christmas! And *adios*!'

Then Blood started to usher everyone towards the exit. 'Now, Sunday, I left your dad around the side of the building,' he said apologetically. 'He may have a lump on his head, but …'

'I will cure him of his condition,' said Jicaque. He placed a hand on Tom's shoulder. 'Just as I will cure you of yours.'

'It takes a lunar month,' Tom said to Sunday.

'And it works, too,' said Stacy, sounding just a little surprised. 'Even I have to admit that.'

Kate felt Tom's hand slide into hers and squeeze reassuringly.

'It may not be all over yet,' he said softly. 'But it's the beginning of the end.'

She wiped her eyes and looked at him. *I must look terrible*, she thought, still stunned by everything they'd just come through. *A total mess.*

But from the way Tom was looking at her, he didn't seem to think so.

'Right then,' said Blood briskly, hanging his jacket over Tom's bare shoulders as they reached the stairwell. 'It's time to play "How many people can we fit in a Mercedes?" Stacy, you can sit on my lap …'

They went outside. The night was cold and the air clear and crisp. Distant revellers toasted Christmas with drunken cheers.

Kate remembered her dad's last words: *'Farewell too to my daughter. May her life be better from this day on.'*

The moon was full and round, high up above the skyscrapers.

I'm not afraid of you anymore, Kate thought.

CHAPTER TWENTY-ONE

'Here you go, Anderson,' said Blood, passing him the tickets. 'May Santa's gift of domestic air travel be yours this Christmas.'

Tom thanked him with a rueful smile. 'Last year for Christmas, I got a Wii and a ton of cool games. This year, it's his and hers tickets to Seattle and a cure for being a werewolf!'

Kate grinned. 'I'm sure Jicaque could maybe upgrade his gift to some comic books and a skateboard if you asked real nice.'

'It is my experience,' said Jicaque gravely, 'that skateboarders can be just as dangerous as werewolves ...'

Tom laughed. He couldn't remember ever feeling so good. A great weight had fallen from his shoulders after all these long months of crawling about in the darkness. Now the sunlight streamed in, warm and dazzling through the concourse windows at O'Hare airport, and it felt unbelievably good against Tom's skin.

It was the day after Boxing Day, and a time for goodbyes.

He and Kate were heading to her old house to go grab the evidence that could clear their names – then they were coming back to Chicago. They would be staying with Sunday and her dad; she'd insisted, and since Jicaque was treating both Tom and Walker together, it seemed to make sense.

'See you tomorrow,' said Sunday, kissing Tom's cheek and almost crushing Kate with a tight hug. 'I'll get your room all ready.' She looked at them mischievously. 'You're gonna be OK sharing, right?'

Tom glanced at Kate and blushed. 'We'll see how it goes.'

Chung stepped forwards and shook Tom's hand. 'Look, man, I've got to split. See you around, OK?'

'You're really going through with it?' marvelled Kate, shaking his hand in turn. 'I mean … China?'

'With the Chapter finished and all my friends dead …' He shrugged. 'In 1875, my family came over from China to Chicago. Now I just feel it's time I went back to the old country. Roots, I guess. You know?'

Jicaque nodded. 'I have many friends in China, old and wise. If you wished—'

'Thanks,' said Chung. 'But I think I should find my own friends. And my own wisdom.'

'That sounds pretty wise of you, for starters,' said Blood amicably, clapping Chung on the back. 'Good luck.'

Chung nodded round at them all. 'Goodbye.' Then he turned and walked away, heading for International Departures.

Blood turned to Stacy and smiled. 'See how easily he's doing that? Just upping sticks and getting away from it all …'

Stacy sighed. 'Adam, we've been through this already …'

'I know, but you're a stubborn little hussy, aren't you?'

'What's all this?' Tom asked, smiling.

'She's so dutiful,' moaned Blood. 'She's got a stack of holiday leave built up and yet she won't come away with me for a little luxury break in Hawaii ...'

Kate frowned at Stacy. 'Are you crazy?'

'But they're so short-staffed at the hospital,' protested Stacy. 'I can't just—'

'Of course you can,' said Blood. 'Tell them you have to go to Hawaii because ... because your sister's really sick.'

'I don't have a sister.'

'Family secret – you just found out about her and you *have* to go.' He beamed over at Tom and Kate. 'Good luck, you two.'

'Yeah,' said Stacy weakly. 'And I'll need some too, with him around!' She tilted her head towards Blood.

'Will you still be here when we get back tomorrow?' asked Kate.

'Sure,' nodded Stacy.

Blood smiled. 'Unless we're in Hawaii, of course.'

'Will you quit with the Hawaii stuff?' complained Stacy, but there was no disguising the grin on her face. 'See you, guys.'

'I've got it! You're investigating the terrifying tropical beach bug ...' Blood steered Stacy away in the direction of the ticket desks, and winked at Tom and Kate. 'Oh, a nasty little virus that one. Lives only in Hawaii, in the whitest possible sands. Think how your colleagues will respect you for finding a cure ...'

Tom watched them walk away, then turned to Kate who was checking her watch.

'We should be going,' she said, then looked up at

Sunday and Jicaque. 'Thanks for everything, guys.'

'May your journey be swift and peaceful,' said Jicaque.

'And with no screaming babies or snoring old men sitting behind you,' added Sunday with a smile.

With a last wave, Tom and Kate headed off to catch the American Eagle internal flight to Seattle.

'Well,' Kate said, as she walked in through the familiar front door. 'This is kind of weird.'

'You're telling me,' Tom replied quietly.

The taxi had dropped them at the causeway that led up to Kate's old house, and she and Tom had walked the rest of the way. The river on either side of them flowed lazily, dreamily. Frost made the conifers sparkle. The sky was darkening like a bruise above them, and Kate started feeling nervous and edgy as they approached the place that had been home since she was fifteen years old.

She flicked on the lights and saw Tom survey the spacious living room suspiciously, as if expecting something nasty to come crawling out of the shadows. But there were only the bleached walls and floorboards, the exposed beams of the high ceiling, her dad's books stacked messily on the bookcases and a dead fire in the grate ...

'This is where it all began,' murmured Tom.

Kate watched him walk over to the place where he'd turned 'wolf for the first time ... the place where her brother had died. A dark, stubborn stain on the polished wood was all that remained of Wesley in the cold, empty house. That all seemed like years ago now, not just a few months.

After she'd found what she was looking for in the pile of mail by the front door, she crossed the room to join Tom. 'Here.' She pressed a padded envelope into his hands.

'The evidence?' he asked.

'Must be. It's Dad's handwriting, and addressed to himself.' She opened it to be sure. 'Yeah ... a CD, and a letter to that lupine in the FBI ...'

'You realise that with this evidence, if we're smart we could actually expose the 'wolves,' Tom said quietly. 'Make normal people accept these things exist.'

'And then destroy them?' Kate shook her head. 'If we start a worldwide 'wolf hunt, there could be worse carnage than the limited killing that goes on now. The lupines would *have* to band together then, to survive. It could mean all-out war ... I won't have that on my conscience.'

Tom sighed. 'I guess so. But we know Takapa's disciples learned something of the codechanters' magics ... we know that all Takapa's research is still sitting there in his warehouse ... So what's to stop the 'wolves just starting again?'

Kate touched his arm. 'Takapa is dead. His 'wolves will have no focus and no cash. And after that whole display at the Bane Gallery, do you think the pure-blood community will be lining up to associate themselves with *anything* he achieved?'

Tom looked at her and half-smiled. 'Then ... we might really have won?'

Kate gave him a tentative smile in return. 'Seems impossible to believe, doesn't it?'

'Time will tell, I guess,' Tom agreed. 'I can't wait for this next month to be over so I can see my family. As plain old Tom Anderson again.'

Kate stared at the smear on the floorboards. 'I've got no family left at all now.'

He looked awkward. 'You only have Blood's word for it that your mom—'

'Don't,' Kate told him. 'You saw the state of her.'

'I'm sorry.'

They stood in silence for some time.

'You know …' Tom sounded awkward. 'You'd be very welcome – more than welcome – to come to my folks' place with me.'

Kate didn't look up. 'That's sweet. But you don't have to do that.'

'I know I don't. I just really want you to meet them.'

'Well, let's wait and see,' Kate said. 'There's still another month to go before you're cured.'

Tom looked at her uncertainly. 'You'll really wait with me until Jicaque's finished?'

She took hold of his fingers. 'Someone's got to hold your hand, right?'

He grinned bashfully. 'Right.'

'Always assuming we can cope with being squeezed into Sunday's spare room together for thirty days.'

'Oh,' Tom said, rubbing his thumb over her finger-tips. 'I think we'll cope.' He paused. 'You know, I'm beat, and the flight back is killer early. Maybe we should think about getting some sleep.'

'Maybe we should,' Kate agreed.

'Uh … where are we sleeping?'

Kate shrugged. 'You can take your pick. And that includes my old bed.' She looked at him. 'I'm not the girl who used to sleep there anymore. Guess I'll take the couch.'

'Well,' Tom said. 'It would be kind of weird, staying in that bedroom with the ghost of the old you. And I'm not exactly dying to stay in that spare bedroom I was held in before.'

She tutted. 'Fussy, aren't you?'

'Uh-huh,' he smiled. 'I can't say I really want to sleep in your mom and dad's bed either ... or your brother's come to that.'

Kate looked at him. 'Guess you're down here with me, then.'

'Guess I am,' Tom said. He took a step towards her and opened his arms.

She met his embrace, sliding her own arms around his neck as he pulled her in close.

This isn't how it ends, she thought. *It's how it begins*.

THE WERELING
TRILOGY

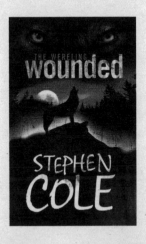

ALSO BY
STEPHEN COLE
THE THIEVES TRILOGY